DAUGHTERS OF TH

Little Mission
on the Clearwater

A STORY BASED ON THE LIFE
OF YOUNG ELIZA SPALDING

Wendy Lawton

MOODY PUBLISHERS
CHICAGO

© 2021 by
WENDY LAWTON

All rights reserved. No part of this book may be reproduced in any form without permission in writing from the publisher, except in the case of brief quotations embodied in critical articles or reviews.

All Scripture is taken from the King James Version.

All emphasis in Scripture has been added.

Published in association with Books & Such Literary Management.

Edited by Pamela Joy Pugh
Interior design: Erik M. Peterson
Cover design: Jeff Miller, Faceout Studio
Cover illustration and portrait: Kelsey Fehlberg
Cover watercolor wash 1 copyright © 2021 by 8H/Shutterstock (1720194910).
Cover watercolor wash 2 copyright © 2021 by TairA/Shutterstock (274620503).
Cover texture copyright © 2021 by titoOnz/Shutterstock (713253826).
All rights reserved for all of the above backgrounds/textures.

Library of Congress Cataloging-in-Publication Data

Names: Lawton, Wendy, author.
Title: Little mission on the Clearwater : a story based on the life of
   young Eliza Spalding / Wendy Lawton.
Description: Chicago : Moody Publishers, 2021. | Series: Daughters of the
   faith ; 9 | Summary: Eliza Spalding lives with her missionary family in
   1847 Oregon, but when an epidemic ravishes the local Indian tribes,
   tensions rise and Eliza witnesses the Whitman Massacre.
Identifiers: LCCN 2021026387 (print) | LCCN 2021026388 (ebook) | ISBN
   9780802424945 (paperback) | ISBN 9780802477880 (ebook)
Subjects: LCSH: Spalding, Eliza Hart, 1807-1851--Juvenile fiction. | CYAC:
   Spalding, Eliza Hart, 1807-1851--Fiction. | Missions--Fiction. |
   Christian life--Fiction. | Nez Percé Indians--Fiction. | Cayuse
   Indians--Fiction. | Frontier and pioneer life--Fiction. | Whitman
   Massacre, 1847--Fiction. | Oregon Territory--History--Fiction. | BISAC:
   JUVENILE FICTION / Historical / General | JUVENILE FICTION / Historical
   / United States / 19th Century | LCGFT: Biographical fiction. |
   Historical fiction.
Classification: LCC PZ7.L4425 Li 2021 (print) | LCC PZ7.L4425 (ebook) |
   DDC [Fic]--dc23
LC record available at https://lccn.loc.gov/2021026387
LC ebook record available at https://lccn.loc.gov/2021026388

Printed by Bethany Press in Bloomington, MN—11/2021

Originally delivered by fleets of horse-drawn wagons, the affordable paperbacks from D. L. Moody's publishing house resourced the church and served everyday people. Now, after more than 125 years of publishing and ministry, Moody Publishers' mission remains the same—even if our delivery systems have changed a bit. For more information on other books (and resources) created from a biblical perspective, go to www.moodypublishers.com or write to

Moody Publishers
820 N. LaSalle Boulevard
Chicago, IL 60610

1 3 5 7 9 10 8 6 4 2

Printed in the United States of America

Contents

1

Little House in the Rye

November 15, 1846
Sexliwal—Deer-Running Season

Why, Mrs. Spalding, I declare, that child is the next thing to a pure savage herself."

Eliza pulled back behind the door so the two women couldn't see that she'd been listening. She knew without having to look that her mother would wince at the word "savage."

"Mrs. Willard," Mama began in her soft voice, folding her apron in her lap. "We work here among the Nez Perce. If we are to bring them the gospel, we must be ever sensible of their ways. We were not called to school the Nez Perce in what they call 'white man ways.'"

"I don't know how you do your missionary work, but I do know something about raising girls, even out here in the wilderness." She took a deep breath as if storing up enough air for a sermon. "Girls should be taught the womanly household arts—sewing, cooking, cleaning, fancywork, maybe a little music and drawing." She made a *harrumph* that resonated loudly. "Even here in this God-forsaken place."

Eliza crept backward on bare feet as she slipped through the door to the yard. God had not forsaken this place and she knew her mother would gently make that point to Mrs. Willard. She silently thanked Noah, her Nez Perce *Yat'sa*—big brother—for teaching her how to move without a sound, like an Indian. It made for a safe escape sometimes.

Mama always said that eavesdroppers hear no good of themselves, but Mrs. Willard's comments echoed what many travelers said about her. Was she growing up wild?

As she moved into the yard, she looked out at the fields surrounding the mission. Most visitors couldn't believe what the Spaldings had accomplished in ten years. When her mother and father had chosen Lapwai as their mission station, there was nothing but grasslands as far as the eye could see.

Now they had a cozy log house, several outbuildings, a gristmill, a print shop, and acres of cultivated fields, a garden, and orchards. Papa said it was important to farm their own land if they were to help the Nez Perce learn to farm.

The vegetable garden was nearly spent for the season. The only remaining plants were pumpkins and squash. This year the garden produced bushels of vegetables. Mama put up as many of the vegetables as she could. She used every crock they owned, including the cracked one, filling them with brined vegetables and sealing each one with wax. She waxed brown paper and tied it over the top of each crock before putting them in storage. She had even traded fresh vegetables at the fort for some new glass jars with tin lids and filled those as well. She salted down some of the vegetables and dried others. The smell of vinegar from the crocks of pickles lasted for days and, at first, made Eliza's nose itch every time she came into the house.

The apple orchard still hung heavy with fruit. Apples kept well for a long time, so Mama didn't have to preserve them in crocks. Barley chaff had already been spread thick on the floor of the root cellar. The apples would be piled onto it when the last of them had been harvested. Papa and his workers would then cover them with more chaff and chopped straw, poking the straw into all the crevices. Papa insisted that they pile at least two feet of chaff on top of the apples to protect them from freezing. The last step was to cover the whole pile in soft moss. Then the apples would keep well into the spring. When the weather warmed up, Mama would dry whatever was left.

All winter long they were able to give gifts of apples to visitors. Nothing is so appreciated, Mama would always say, as fresh fruit in the middle of winter. It was Eliza's job to go to the root cellar to fetch apples out of the pile, but she wished she could talk her brother, Henry, into doing it. Every time she opened the door she heard scurrying sounds. And each time she pushed her arm into the pile to extract an apple, she half expected a mouse to surprise her.

The rest of the fields around the mission were already harvested. The wheat and barley had been cut, ground into flour, and stored. Just beyond the fields were miles and miles of rye grass. During the hot months of the year it turned brown and dry. Mama always worried about fire danger, but Eliza loved the dry grasses. When the wind blew, the grass rustled, sounding like soft murmurs. When she was little, Eliza believed the rye told secrets. If she could just listen hard enough, she could eavesdrop on those secrets. Sometimes it sounded like they were just whispering "shhhh," over and over again.

A sound from the building that housed the printing press caught her attention—the clack, clack, clack of Papa setting type. It was a Saturday, so Mama didn't have school or have the Nez Perce women coming for needlework lessons. This past year Mama often saw close to two hundred adults and children in the schoolroom Papa and the other men had built. Only on Saturday did Mama have time for visitors or doing household chores. On the Sabbath they held services for the Nez Perce in the schoolroom.

Papa worked on Saturdays just like every other day. His favorite place to work was at the printing press. As he so often reminded them, how many young mission stations in the wilderness have a printing press? The native peoples of the church of Honolulu had sent it from the far-off Sandwich Islands as a gift to the mission. Eliza liked to think about how far it had traveled to come to them. It came on a freighter across the ocean and then was shipped by barge up the Columbia

Gorge and finally carried over land by wagon to the mission. The printing press meant that the Nez Perce could have books printed in their own language. Little by little they would have the Bible and, because of the mission school, they could soon read it themselves.

Every chance he got, Papa set type and printed pages. He worked quickly with a click, click, click as each piece of movable type was slid into place on the frame. Papa had to put every single letter in the proper order for each page.

"Papa?"

Her father stopped and smiled at her. "All alone, 'Liza? You are usually trailing Henry or Noah."

"Noah hasn't come today. Maybe he's working with the horses." She pulled up a stool close to the table where her father worked. "Henry is minding Martha Jane today since Mama has a visitor."

"Hmmm." Her father put his hand on the open page of the Bible and pulled his handwritten pages closer and began to fill the type tray again.

"Do you think I'm wild?"

He looked up. "Why would you ask that?"

She didn't know how to answer. She shouldn't have been eavesdropping on Mama and Mrs. Willard. She took a letter E out of the letter case. She pressed it into the skin of her hand, leaving the imprint of the letter on her hand.

"Why did you name me Eliza?" She knew her father was used to her changing the subject.

"You know the story. I wanted to name you for your mother."

"Two Elizas in one family." She breathed in the smell of paper and ink. "Will I ever be like Mama?"

Papa set the tray aside and took her hand. "I can tell something is bothering you." He looked at her for a long minute. "Your mother is an extraordinary woman. Along with Mrs. Whitman she was the first white woman to cross the Continental Divide." He smiled. "Think about it. They were the first white women in the whole of the Oregon territory." He was quiet again. "But you are a pioneer just like your mother."

Eliza knew that story. She begged her mother to tell parts of it whenever there was time in the evening. That wasn't what she meant. Her mother could draw and paint. The Nez Perce loved her drawings. Her needlework was the finest in the territory. The settlers who visited always commented on it. She cooked, gardened, taught Indian School, taught the Nez Perce women, and took care of her family.

"Does this have to do with being wild?" her father asked.

She nodded.

"You are not wild. Your mother and I came to this territory to bring Jesus to the Nez Perce Indians. We wanted to teach them some of the things we knew, like farming and needlework. But we also wanted to learn from them."

"Like all you know about horses?"

"Yes, but that's just one thing. I think I've learned far more from our Nez Perce friends than they've learned from us." He turned back to the letter case and Eliza moved her stool closer. "It is more important to us that you learn from the Nez Perce than that you turn a fine seam or study watercolors—at least for now."

Eliza thought about that. So that was why Mama and Papa allowed her to spend so much time with Timothy and Matilda in the Nez Perce village and play with her friend Noah.

"Do you know how many white settlers can speak Nez Perce?" He didn't wait for her answer. "Precious few. But you not only speak the language, you've helped me fashion a written language so we can give our friends the Bible in their own language."

Eliza breathed in deeply through her nose. Maybe what looked like wildness was being the good missionary her father always said they must be.

Her father continued to set type.

"Would it help if I read the passage to you while you set the type?"

"It would. I could go much faster. Then I'll just have to double-check our spelling and punctuation when I'm finished. I'm redoing Genesis since we refined some of the spelling. Start at 1:1."

She picked up his paper and started to read slowly. "*Uyít-pa Akamkiniku-m pa-háni-a uág uétas-na, kauá kuníg pa-háni-a úikala-na petú-na úilákz-zíkiú uéutukt.*"

"Good. I have that correct. Now continue."

Eliza read the passage until he finished the form. He then

took the paper she had been reading and checked each word against the type he had set. "There," he said, "we're ready to go."

She watched him put the form on the bed of the press and ink the type. He put the paper between the two frames—her father called them the frisket and the tympan—and rolled the bed into place. She loved to see the paper press against the type, knowing the words would print on the paper. Papa took the paper off and hung it on a wire to dry while he repeated the process to print page after page.

In the beginning, God created the heaven and the earth. This was a lesson the Nez Perce already knew. They knew about the Creator long before the white trappers had come. And they knew about the Bible before her parents had ever decided to come to the Oregon territory. She loved that story.

As her father worked the press she wandered out into the yard. It was a beautiful, cool fall morning. The last of the leaves on the trees still showed color. When the sun shone, like today, the color took one's breath away.

Several Nez Perce stood outside the makeshift gristmill with grain or sacks of flour. Timothy stood in the middle of the men. She ran toward him. Timothy was one of the first believers at the mission. He stood tall even among the Nez Perce. His hair was mostly black, tied back in a thong of rawhide. The gray color along his temples was the sign of an elder—a respected one. Even since before she was born, Timothy had been one of her family's closest friends. He helped her father learn the language and encouraged his people to come to the mission.

As she drew near, she heard Timothy speaking with another man. She knew it was impolite to interrupt, so she stood waiting nearby. She could hear most of the conversation. It was about the Cayuse over at *Wai-i-lat-pu*—the Whitman mission. She'd been there many times.

When her parents came west, there was another missionary couple with them, the Whitmans. They settled near Fort Walla Walla on the Oregon Trail to work among the Cayuse. Mama and Papa continued on and set up their mission near Lapwai, the home of the Nez Perce. Secretly, Eliza was glad. She loved the Nez Perce people. From the earliest time—some say the days of the Spaniards—they had been horse breeders and were respected by most of the tribes. Their horses were the best. Papa always said he'd take a Nez Perce pony over an eastern Thoroughbred any day.

She sighed just thinking about their horses.

Eliza loved horses. Noah had a pony and sometimes he let her ride. But she longed for a pony of her own. She even had a name picked out—*Ayi*—if she ever got a pony. Every time she asked Papa about it, he'd answer, "In due time, Eliza. In due time." If only he'd say "in six months," or in "one year," she could count off the days, but "in due time"? What did that mean? Sometimes she pretended he'd said dew time. When she woke up to dew on the ground, like this morning, she'd think, maybe today is the day Ayi will come. But so far, the dew never brought Ayi.

She watched the men talking. Timothy mostly listened. She couldn't hear it all but she heard enough to worry her. The short man talked of jealousy and unrest. He said the Cayuse were concerned about the growing numbers of white settlers that crossed through their land on the Oregon Trail. Because the settlers stopped at the Whitman Mission, they believed the mission was bringing the people to take over Cayuse land.

Timothy said little but he promised the man that he'd speak to Eliza's father about it.

When Timothy turned and saw her, a smile broke on his worried face. "Little one, have you come to say *Tats Meywi* to Timothy?"

"*Tats Meywi, Piimx.* Good morning. Are you grinding wheat today?" She and Henry called Timothy *Piimx*—uncle—out of respect.

"Yes. Last grain before snows come."

"Timothy," she hesitated. Should she mention the conversation she'd overheard? "Are the Cayuse angry with us?"

"Not you, little one. Much change in the land. I talk with your father."

Eliza wished she could listen in. She didn't know why everyone couldn't just get along. Whenever people argued, it made her stomach hurt. But surely Timothy and her father could work this out.

"You see Noah today?" Timothy asked.

"He hasn't come."

"You ride back to village with me. Special day. Henry, too."

It was a special day—her birthday. Today she was nine years old.

She ran to ask her mother. As she entered the house, Mrs. Willard seemed to be taking leave so Eliza moved to her corner of the house and pulled on stockings and her sturdy boots. Even though it was November, she often still wore her moccasins around the mission grounds. The dirt was packed too tight for grass to grow so she didn't have to worry about hidden snakes, and she rarely stayed in one place long enough for her feet to get cold. But if she were going to the Nez Perce village, she'd need her shoes and stockings.

Her brother, Henry, had been minding Martha Jane. She had only been walking for about six months but she could get into everything. Henry was almost seven years old and there was nothing he liked better than playing with the baby. He and Eliza took turns watching her while Mama taught Indian School or entertained visitors, but Henry was happiest when it was his turn. He would put a stocking over his hand and play puppets with Martha for hours.

This morning he'd worn the baby out. She slept on a pile of quilts in the corner.

Eliza whispered, "Timothy will take us to the village if Mama lets us go."

Henry didn't need convincing. He sat down and pulled on his stockings and boots as well. "What are we going to do?"

"I don't know. Let's see what Noah is doing."

Mama came in after seeing Mrs. Willard off. "What are you two planning?" she asked with a smile.

"Timothy is over at the gristmill but he said he'd take us to the village when he's ready to leave. Can we go?"

"I cannot see any reason for you not to go, especially since I have something special to do this afternoon."

Before Eliza could ask about this special task, her mother continued. "Your father is going to the village to meet with some of the men later this afternoon, so he will bring you back home." Her mother turned to get her sewing basket. "Will you take this floss to Matilda?" She handed Eliza a card with a sunny yellow thread wound 'round.

Eliza took the thread and tucked it deep into the pocket of her apron.

"Now have a little food before you go." She cut slices of bread off the loaf she baked the day before and spread some of her berry preserves on them. She poured two cups of fresh milk to go with the bread.

While they sat at the table to eat, Mama left to take food out to Papa so he didn't have to stop working. On days like these when noonday dinner was quick, they often had their warm meal at suppertime.

As Eliza rushed through the small meal, her mind flitted in different directions. Should she be worried about angry Cayuse or about the settlers thinking her wild or about the special task her mother needed to do?

It was her birthday. She'd think about secrets. The rest could wait for another day.

A Day to Remember

November 15, 1846
Sexliwal—Deer-Running Season

T hey rode to the village on Timothy's horse, Henry in front and Eliza in back. She hung on tightly as Timothy fairly flew across the prairie. He rarely spoke, but that was his way. They were used to his silence. They passed a field where the Nez Perce threshed the last of their wheat in a whirlwind of dust and snorting horses. Timothy's horse sidestepped the chaos.

Eliza's father said the Indians threshed their grain unlike anyone back in the States. They formed a yard of wheat stacks and brought in fifteen or twenty wild horses. The horses ran through the stacks, trampling the wheat right on the ground until there was nothing left but chaff. They didn't even rake off. At night, when the wind came up, the women would come out with fans made from willows, and then the winnowing began.

In the end, the grain would be gathered up and taken to the gristmill at the mission to be ground into flour. It was a sight to see.

As they neared the village, Eliza heard the familiar sounds—dogs barking, children shrieking, and horses nickering. The aromas welcomed them—wood smoke, dust, buffalo meat drying over a smoky fire, and the earthy smell of reeds being soaked in water.

"Eliza! Henry!" Noah came running toward them. "I've been waiting for you."

"How did you know we were coming?" Eliza asked as she slid off the horse, onto the ground. Timothy handed Henry to one of the men who came to take his horse. As Timothy got off the horse, she saw him look at Noah and press his lips tight.

"Come. See Matilda." Noah was one or two years older than Eliza. Her Nez Perce *Yat'sa*, besides teaching her how to track, had taught her to ride and to care for horses.

They didn't need any urging to visit Matilda. She was like family to them. Eliza had never met her own grandmother and grandfather. They lived far back in the States—in New York. She didn't know what it felt like to have a grandmother, but she often thought it must feel like being with Matilda.

Matilda didn't have any children of her own left. She never spoke about it but Mama said they must have died. Eliza knew Matilda was old by the way her people respected her, but she was as strong as the young women in the village. Maybe stronger.

As they neared her teepee, they saw Matilda sitting outside on a log by her cooking fire minding three babies tied to cradleboards.

Noah ran up to her. "I've brought Eliza and Henry to you."

Henry hugged Matilda. Eliza hugged her as well and gave her the floss from Mama.

She smiled. "Come. Sit." She pointed to another log. "Papoose must stay with Matilda. The mothers winnow after threshing." Eliza loved to talk with Matilda, who spoke English as well as almost anyone, even if she left out some words, like "a" or "the." All her Nez Perce friends spoke English this way since they didn't have those words in their own language.

Now Eliza reached out toward the baby, who was awake. The elaborately decorated cradleboard fascinated her. Babies always seemed content being wrapped tightly to the board. She propped the board against the log so this baby could look at Matilda instead of just the sky above. Sometimes when she visited the village she would see a cradleboard hung on a pole so the baby could watch his or her mama at work or see all around the village.

"Just think, Eliza, how easy it would be to watch Martha Jane if we could strap her into a cradleboard," Henry said.

Eliza laughed. "Martha Jane is walking now so she's too big for a cradleboard." She turned toward Matilda. "Henry spent the morning keeping her out of trouble for Mama."

Matilda smiled at Henry.

"She runs so fast now I can hardly keep up with her," Henry said.

"I don't think she'd be happy tied to a cradleboard. Besides, look at how long it would take to unlace her to change her diapers."

"On cradleboard, no need to change diapers," Matilda said shrugging her shoulders. "We wrap cloth around clump of dry peat moss and put in with papoose. Keeps wet from baby all day."

Eliza laughed. Leave it to the Nez Perce to come up with a better diaper. The cradleboards themselves were works of art. Her father had traded for many pieces of Nez Perce art, including cradleboards, and sent them back to mission officials.

Matilda saw her staring at the cradleboard. "Cradleboard makes children feel safe—wrapped tightly."

Eliza had to agree. She had never seen a fussy Nez Perce baby on a cradleboard. She traced the intricate design with her finger.

"Cradleboard come from Joseph family."

Mama had told Eliza that cradleboards were passed down from generation to generation. The braver the man who had been reared on the cradleboard, the more in demand it was. This cradleboard must have been for *Hin-mah-too-yah-lat-kekht,* the son of Joseph the Elder, chief of the Wallowa Nez Perce. Noah met the chief's son on an elk hunt and had told Eliza about him. He was already much admired. They called him Joseph, like his father.

When a Nez Perce became a Christian they chose an English name, like Timothy, Matilda, and Noah had. They also kept the Nez Perce name they had been given, which reflected their personality, physical skills, or characteristics. They didn't receive that name from their parents until they were about six or seven. Until then they were just referred to as "little one" or "my baby" in the Nez Perce language. No one believed they could come up with the right name for a person until they understood him or her well enough.

"Today is Eliza's birthday," Henry said.

"How did you know that?" Eliza asked. Birthdays were celebrated quietly in her home, usually with something sweet at supper—maybe a cake if the hens were laying— and a small gift. But it wasn't suppertime yet, so how did Henry know?

"I just know," Henry said.

"I know, too." Noah said. "But I cannot say more."

Hmmm. So many secrets.

"I have gift for you, my friend." Matilda handed her a soft buffalo hide pouch.

Eliza didn't know what to say. She had never received a gift from one of her Nez Perce friends. She thought about gifts her mother had given to Timothy or others. What had they said to thank her?

"I am honored, *Kat'sa*." She lowered her head.

"Open it, 'Liza," Henry said. "Open it."

Matilda smiled as Eliza opened the rawhide drawstring. Beads! The pouch had dozens of beads inside. Most were seed beads strung on thin sinews to keep the tiny glass beads together. These were used in creating the intricate designs Matilda beaded onto camas bags and dresses. Eliza ran her fingers through the cool glass beads and pulled out the larger ones. There were three blue Lewis and Clark beads. These were her mother's favorites. There were several watermelon beads as well. These oblong beads looked like a ripe watermelon—striped green on the outside with a red center where the hole pierced. There were also a number of turquoise beads.

"Oh, *Kat'sa!*" Eliza threw her arms around the older woman. She knew how valuable these beads were. The craftsmen of the tribe treasured their beads. They had been used as a form of money—trade beads—for years as the Indians traded furs to the trappers in exchange for beads.

"Your mother wishes you to learn needlework like white women learn." She leaned back and laughed. "Matilda thinks you can include *Nimiipuu* designs in needlework."

"I will." Eliza could picture the designs she'd like to make.

Matilda took the pouch and pulled out the brown seed beads. They reminded Eliza of sarsaparilla that Papa brought back from a trip to Fort Vancouver.

Matilda held the string of beads up to the light. "Color of earth warmed by sun. And color of Eliza's hair." She reached into the pouch again and brought out some of the Russian blues. "Color of sky. Color of Eliza's eyes."

She put the beads back into the pouch and pulled the drawstring tight. Eliza took the pouch and tucked it deep into her apron pocket. She wanted to thank Matilda again for the gift but she knew she must not. One thank you was enough. More might seem insincere.

"There's Papa." Henry pointed toward the wigwam where their father dismounted from his horse and went inside to talk with the elders. Were they talking about the angry Cayuse?

The wigwam was the gathering place in the village. It was long and rectangular, made of a framework of poles covered with reed mats. The roof was sod, cut right from the fields. With a fire lit inside it was warmer than a log home.

The other homes in the village were teepees. These were made of poles, spread out in a wide circle at the bottom and lashed together at the top. Hides covered the poles. Many of the teepees had colorful scenes or designs painted on them. The people kept the teepees cool in the hot season by rolling up the hides and letting the breezes blow through the bottom of the teepee. They kept the teepee warm in winter by bringing the fire inside and keeping the sides down. The smoke from the fire escaped through the opening at the top where the poles came together. In wintertime, the snowy village was dotted with teepees, laced tight against the cold with a thin plume of smoke rising from the top of each one.

Noah said the teepees made it easy to move the entire village for hunting or for gathering camas root.

When the mission first came, her father urged the Nez Perce to stay in one place and farm as well as hunt. Many of the braves resisted, saying digging in the dirt was for women, but after one or two harvests, they objected less. Grain could be stored for the time when game became scarce. The women still did much of the farming.

Papa said that besides wanting the Nez Perce to be well fed, if they stayed in one place they could attend services on the Sabbath and regularly attend school. It's hard to build friendships, he would always say, if people never stay in one place.

Eliza wondered why her family didn't just get a teepee and follow the tribe.

Eliza, Noah, and Henry spent the afternoon helping Matilda take the babies to their mothers for feeding, turning the pieces of Chinook salmon that were drying on racks in the sun, and visiting the litter of puppies that had been born in a jumble of fallen trees down by the river.

They came back into the village just as their father came out of the wigwam. He nodded at Noah. "Are you ready to go home?" he asked Eliza and Henry.

Noah had taken off without even saying goodbye.

"Can Noah come home with us?" Eliza asked.

"Not today. We have someone else to take home with us tonight."

"Someone else?" Eliza didn't understand. It couldn't be Matilda because she was minding babies. Who—

"'Liza, you are nine years old today. Your mother and I decided it was old enough for you to take care of your own pony."

Noah came out from behind the wigwam leading a beautiful little pinto pony.

For a moment, Eliza couldn't speak. She had dreamed of her own horse. Could it be true? The pony tossed her head and nickered softly.

"*Ayi!*" Eliza ran over and threw her arms around the pony's neck. In all her daydreams she had never pictured one as beautiful as this.

"I trained her myself," Noah said. Although he was still a boy, everyone acknowledged his skill with horses.

"Thank you, Papa. Thank you, Noah." She could barely get the words out. A horse. She had her own horse. She ran her hands over Ayi's hindquarters, which wore patches of white running through the warm sorrel color. A beautifully woven Nez Perce blanket covered Ayi's back and an Indian saddle rested on it.

She looked over at Matilda's teepee. She and Timothy stood smiling. Everyone must have known but her.

"Are you ready to ride?" Papa helped her up into the saddle. "Henry will ride with me."

"When do I get a pony, Papa?" Henry asked.

"In due time, son. In due time."

● ● ●

"Mama, can I go outside and make sure Ayi is comfortable?" Eliza could hardly bear to sit and eat dinner when her very own pony stood just a short way away. On the ride home she'd barely gotten acquainted with her pony but she could already see that Papa had handpicked this one for her. As she talked to Ayi, the horse pricked her ears and seemed to be trying to learn Eliza's strange language.

"Eliza, I cooked your favorites for supper tonight. Your horse will still be there in the morning." Mama had cooked elk stew and baking powder biscuits. The stew was rich with potatoes, carrots, celery, parsnips, and onions.

"A delicious meal, Mrs. Spalding." Papa always called Mama by her married name. And she called him Reverend Spalding. When they said it, it sounded like pet names—special names. "And a little birdie told me we have Scripture cake for dessert."

Martha Jane, sitting on a stack of books, chirped, "Birdie, birdie."

Henry laughed out loud. "She's getting old enough to join in the dinner conversation."

"I hope we have Burnt Jeremiah syrup for the cake," Eliza said. Scripture cake with syrup was her favorite.

"Surely you can smell it." Mama took a deep breath in through her nose, which started a coughing fit.

Eliza caught the worried look on Papa's face before he masked it with a smile. "I smelled it as soon as we walked in the door."

"Birdie, birdie," the baby said.

"It's a good thing Martha Jane is getting older," Mama said as soon as her coughing subsided. "I have a feeling a new baby may be joining us before Christmas."

"A new baby!" Henry jumped up from the table to hug his mother. "Can I help take care of the baby?"

"I will need all of your help so that I can keep teaching

school and my needlework classes. Not to mention taking good care of the Spalding family."

Eliza knew she would help. Nobody worked as hard as her mother. Of course, nobody enjoyed the work as much. Mama was delighted to have so many students. Usually the house was filled with Nez Perce—even at dinnertime. She always cooked double the portion, knowing they'd likely have visitors. Women from the village often came to prepare a meal with her. The cast iron cook stove fascinated them. Mama learned from them as well. She had a pothook put in the fireplace and often cooked over the open fire as her Nez Perce friends taught her.

As they finished supper, Mama brought the cake to the table and drizzled the syrup over it. Before she cut it, she said, "We have a birthday gift for Eliza."

"But what about Ayi? Isn't she my gift?"

"No. We've been waiting for the right pony to come along for you. It just happened that she was ready on your birthday." Her father folded his hands. "You will use the pony to help us with the mission work—taking things to the village, fetching things from the village."

"And when you go to school you will need a way to get there. It's a hundred and twenty miles to the Whitman mission," Mama said.

Go to school? No one had ever talked about her leaving the Lapwai mission. Leave her family?

Her mother pushed a package across the table. It was wrapped in a piece of brown paper and tied with string. Mama had tucked a colorful fall leaf under the string. "Open it."

Eliza untied the string and smoothed the paper out. Inside was a leather-bound journal, an iron-nib pen, and a jar of ink.

"Oh, Mama. Now I have a journal like yours."

"Your father reminded me that you are living a life unlike almost any girl your age. You are the first girl descended from European roots to grow up in the Oregon territory. You are a true pioneer, and you should keep a record of your life."

Eliza didn't know what to say. She never thought about her life as important—as making history. She ran her hand over the leather.

"One of the settlers said Eliza was the very first white baby born west of the Rockies," Henry said.

"No," said Papa. "Another baby was born earlier but sadly, that little one is no longer with us."

Another baby? How could that be? It couldn't be a brother or sister, could it? The only white women in the whole territory were Mrs. Whitman and Mama. Eliza knew by the expression on her mother's and father's faces that it was a closed subject, and she dared not question further.

"Thank you for the journal and pen." She knew that the first thing she would write about was the mysterious baby.

Before bedtime, Eliza sat at one end of the table across from her mother as they both wrote in their journals, the lantern between them casting long shadows.

Journal of Eliza Spalding, Daughter

Eliza thought she should add the word "daughter" because her mother was also named Eliza Spalding and Mama faithfully kept her journal to record the history of settlers as well.

November 15, 1846

In 1837, on this day, my mother gave birth to me right here at Lapwai. I always believed my birth to be the first non-native birth west of the Rocky Mountains. West of the Continental Divide. I was wrong. Papa says another baby was first. How can that be? The only white women in the territory at that time were Mama and Mrs. Whitman, who has no children. Papa and Mama looked at each other in that mysterious way that always made me long to discover the story behind the mystery.

This was the best day of my life. I not only received the gift of this beautiful journal, but Ayi came into my life. My sweet little pinto pony. I plan to work with her, care for her and, with Noah's help, teach her tricks like the Indian ponies.

Matilda gave me some beautiful beads. I can't decide whether to work them into some leather needlework or just keep them in my little pouch. When I hold the blue beads up to the sun, they look like jewels.

I want to make my journal special, like no one else's journal. I'm not sure how. I shall have to think about that.

I forgot to write that we had Scripture cake, too. Mama always tries to surprise us with something delicious.

To end each day, I shall choose a Bible verse. Today because I was well fed and I received the desire of my heart, I chose Psalm 37:3–4:"Trust in the Lord, and do good; so shalt thou dwell in the land, and verily thou shalt be fed. Delight thyself also in the Lord: and he shall give thee the desires of thine heart." *As I go to sleep, I will delight in the Lord Jesus and also pray we shall be able to dwell in this land safely.*

3

Christmas at Lapwai

December 1846
Haoq'oy—Season of Expectant Doe

Here. Lash this pole to the side of her saddle." Henry threw Eliza a leather thong. "I'll tie the other pole." Henry was always figuring out how to make things.

"Are you sure this won't hurt her?" Eliza ran a hand down Ayi's neck.

"She is used to it. Noah had her pulling travois before you got her." They tied the poles onto a ring on each side of the saddle. "Noah says that Indian ponies like to work."

She'd had her pony for almost a month now and had spent much of every day with her. They had become good friends. Before harvest, Eliza had gathered all the fallen apples that had not been badly bruised. She kept her own pile of apples in the corner of the barn. Ayi liked having apple treats. Each day, when Eliza came into the barn, Ayi would nudge her until she took the apple out of her apron pocket.

Once the makeshift travois was tightly lashed to Ayi, Henry began to lead her toward the stand of lodgepole pines at the far end of the mission grounds. Eliza walked alongside.

"Mama is going to be pleased," she said. Mama often talked about decorating the farmhouse for Christmas in her home-town of Holland Patent far away in New York State when she was a child. She spoke of making evergreen garlands with bit-tersweet berries and draping them on the banister and across the hearth. They had always made a holly wreath for the door. "We'll gather pine boughs and pile them on the travois."

"What about the holly wreath?" Henry asked. "Do we have holly here?"

"I don't think so. Mama has drawn pictures of her holly wreath and I don't think we have anything like that. But there are red hawthorns growing along the Clearwater. The berries are even prettier than Mama's holly berries."

A storm had passed through just a week earlier, so when they got to the stand of trees there were plenty of fresh branches on the ground. They gathered far more than they needed, knowing that the remainder would smell fragrant in the barn, drying for the fireplace.

As they headed toward the Clearwater, they crossed tracks which looked like they had been made by three or four Indian horses. She could always tell if the tracks were from settlers' horses or Indians' horses by the prints. Settlers used iron horseshoes while Indian ponies were unshod. The prints they made were very different.

Off in the distance they could see three Cayuse braves watering their horses. Henry stopped and put his finger across his lips. They knew the Cayuse had seen them—Indians sensed movement more keenly than even trappers and mountain men. But there was no sense in confronting strangers. Had it been Nez Perce it would have been different, but the Cayuse were not their neighbors and friends.

Words carried on the wind. Their language was close enough to Nez Perce that Eliza understood most of what they were saying. One Cayuse mocked the white settlers who let their children have valuable ponies for play. A different voice angrily railed about settlers taking everything that belonged to Cayuse—land, horses, and customs like the travois.

Eliza and Henry stood still. The Cayuse should recognize that it was out of respect that they did not approach them.

When their horses had drunk their fill, the Cayuse mounted, reared their horses in a show of power, and rode off. Eliza realized she'd been holding her breath.

"Why are they angry with us?" Henry asked.

"I don't know. We didn't take their land. The Nez Perce asked us to come and gave us this land." Eliza would talk to Papa about it tonight. It worried her. More than anything, she wanted everyone to live peacefully among one another. Last night her mother had read the passage from Joshua 22 about the monument built by warring tribes before the Lord as a remembrance of the friendship of all the tribes of Israel whether they were east or west of the Jordan River. That was what Eliza longed for in the Oregon territory—friendship of all the tribes and the settlers. Why did that feel so unlikely lately?

"Come, let's get the hawthorn branches and go back home so we can decorate for Christmas."

• • •

Mama laughed and clapped her hands when she came back from the village to find the house decorated. "It smells just like home in New York. I almost expect to walk out the door and hear carolers in the Holland Patent Square." She sat down. She smiled but she was clearly tired. It was less than a fortnight since the birth of baby Amelia but she had insisted on riding to the village to bring a Christmas pudding to Matilda. Now it was time to feed Amelia again.

"Did you like your holly wreath?" Henry asked as Mama fed the baby. Martha Jane stood sucking her thumb by Mama's knee.

"The red hawthorn is even prettier than our holly but I won't tell anyone back in the States. It shall be our secret."

Eliza couldn't stop looking at all the greenery. They had put hawthorn berries in the pine boughs. The red and green looked so festive—just like Mama had described her childhood Christmas.

"Tomorrow we have to get the fires going early so the schoolroom will be warm for all those coming for our Christmas service." She paused. "I wish we had the numbers of worshipers we had just three years ago. Do you remember, Eliza?"

Eliza shook her head.

"In 1843, we had upwards of two thousand people come to worship services. The crowds were so large we had to hold services outdoors."

Eliza remembered outdoor Sabbath services and was just about to say so when Papa came in. He smelled of ink.

"Things are different now, Mrs. Spalding, aren't they?" He went over to the basin and washed his hands. "It doesn't help that Tom Hill settled down to live with the Nez Perce."

"Who's Tom Hill?" Eliza asked.

"He's half white, half Delaware, and full of anger. He's been telling the Nez Perce how the Americans drove his people from one place to another until almost none are left."

"But sadly, much of what he says about the broken treaties is true, isn't it?" Mama asked.

"It is, but he blames it all on religion. Claims to be an expert on what he calls white man's religion and has convinced most of the young men of the tribe."

Papa sat down and looked around the room, noticing it for the first time. "It looks like Christmas back in the States. Am I still in the Oregon territory?"

"Henry and Eliza made a travois, gathered the greens, and surprised me with this."

Papa smiled. "What a nice gift to give to your mother. The house smells like a memory."

Eliza was proud of their work but she couldn't stop thinking about Tom Hill. "Papa, is that man Tom Hill making everyone angry with us?"

"No, 'Liza. Not at all." Papa leaned back. "It's just frustrating that he's had any influence at all. The elders are still our friends. The women admire your mother and call her friend. Even many of the braves—the ones who know Jesus—continue to be friendly toward us."

"But the other ones—the angry ones—are they the ones who've been stealing our tools?" Henry asked. "Are they the ones who broke things in the gristmill?"

"We don't know. Timothy isn't sure if it's Nez Perce or Cayuse who are riding through, looking to cause havoc. Either way, we just have to continue to pray that God will soften hearts again."

"How many do you expect at the Christmas service?" Mama asked.

"I don't know. I have several hundred gifts ready."

Eliza knew what the gifts were. They'd been working on them for nearly a year. It was the gospel of John in the Nez Perce language printed on the mission's very own press. She, Henry, and Noah would get to help give the gifts to each family at the close of the service.

She could hardly wait. That night she wrote:

December 21, 1846
   Tonight, in this journal, I shall write my prayer since I am filled with a confusing mix of great joy and a sense that

something very bad comes before many seasons.

Heavenly Father, I thank You that You know the future and that You guided the past. The Cayuse and other enemies of our faith and our way of living stir up trouble. I sense that the trouble grows bigger and shows no sign of lessening. I long for peace.

And, Lord, thank You for planting that seed in the Nez Perce that caused them to travel long miles to ask us to come to Lapwai. I love the Nez Perce and I love You. Replace my fear with trust.

Psalm 91:5: Thou shalt not be afraid for the terror by night; nor for the arrow that flieth by day.

• • •

Timothy stood tall at the lectern. "Reverend Spalding ask Timothy to tell story of how Bible come to Nez Perce. To the People."

Timothy began his story in his native language. He first told how, many moons ago, when his people were camping for the winter at Weippe, he'd been out scouting for berries and came across a party of pale men with hair on their faces and eyes of glass. He had never seen white men before. He ran back to the camp to tell the elders. They decided the strange men were a danger to their people and must be killed.

Wat-ku-ese, an old woman, lay dying in her teepee. When she heard about the plans for a war party, she asked to speak to the chief and the elders. They helped her to the wigwam where the men were meeting. "Do not kill them," she begged. "These are *Su-i-yap-po*—white men—I told you about." Everyone in the tribe knew she had been captured as a little girl and passed from tribe to tribe before finding herself with a white family. They were kind to her—the first kindness she had ever known. When they were gone, she had made her way back to the Nez Perce.

The elders decided to spare the *Su-i-yap-po*—the Lewis and Clark expedition— as they came over the Lolo trail.

"William Clark first show us his Bible. We call it the White Man's Book of Heaven, but when he left, he took book with him." Timothy held up Papa's Bible.

He continued his story. Many seasons ago, three young Nez Perce men—*H'co-a-h'co-a-h'cotes* (Black Eagle), *Hee-oh-'ks-te-kin* (Rabbit-Skin Leggings), *Tip-ya-lah-na-jah-nim* (No Horns on His Head)—and one Flathead named *Ka-ou-pen* (Man of the Morning) began a journey to learn more about this book. They traveled all the way to St. Louis, the city of the Red-Headed Chief, General William Clark. Black Eagle told him, "My people sent me to get White Man's Book of Heaven."

Eliza loved this story. She looked around the room and saw that everyone was listening intently. They already knew the story—it was part of their history—but they listened as if they were hearing it for the first time.

Timothy continued. "*Nimiipuu* hear about Jesus little here, little there, but deep need to know about Him come from God. Great Father plant hunger in here," he pressed his hands to his chest. "Our people travel far to ask for help." He told how General Clark wrote a letter to the missionary societies back east.

"That how Reverend Spalding come to bring us Book of Heaven—Bible. We ask and he come." Timothy paused to let his words sink in. "We ask and he come."

Timothy went on to tell them how much they'd learned in the ten years the Spaldings had been with them—farming, harvesting, operating a gristmill, reading, needlework, new ways of spinning and weaving and, most importantly, they'd learned about the Bible and could now hear it read in their own language.

"Today we keep *Halkh-pa-wit*, holy day—day of Christ's birth. We celebrate good gifts God give us—Bible, and greatest gift of all, His Son, our Savior." Timothy paused. "Reverend Spalding make gift for each Nez Perce family today." He gestured to Papa to come to the lectern as the excitement level in the room was raised.

Papa bowed his head and prayed in the people's language. He thanked God for letting his family come to live as friends with the Nez Perce and to bring the Bible to them. When he looked up, he signaled to Eliza, Henry, and Noah as they began to sing "O Come, All Ye Faithful."

The three of them passed out the newly printed gospel of John, one to each family. Mama had wrapped each book in a piece of brightly colored calico and tied it with string. There was great excitement in the room. Eliza could tell by the way they received these that this gift would be treasured for a long time to come. She couldn't imagine what it would have been like not to have a Bible to read in your own language.

After all their guests had left, her family went into the house to celebrate their own family Christmas. The smell of wild turkey roasting, mixed with the fragrance of pine boughs, was one Eliza knew she'd never forget.

Mama had made gifts for each one—warm booties for baby Amelia, a rag doll for Martha Jane, a marble sack for Henry, and a warm shawl for Eliza. Dark came early, so the candles were lit before dinner was served.

As they ate, Papa and Mama discussed the day.

"The service was lovely," Mama said.

"Timothy reminded them about God's hand in their tribal history. It reminded me again as well." Papa smiled. "Even I need to be reminded that we didn't come here on a whim. It was God's plan and He is the one who will see it to the end."

Eliza needed to hear that as well. Sometimes, when everyone seemed angry with each other, she needed to remember that God would take care of them.

4

Sham Battle

January 1847
Wilupup—Season of Blizzards

As they came over the hill, Eliza could see thin trails of smoke rising from the center of each teepee in the village. Papa stopped to let the party see the village spread out below. It looked still under its blanket of snow.

"The village is quieter in winter than any other time of year," he said. "Hunting continues and the work of preparing skins and caring for animals never stops, but life for the Nez Perce slows down."

Mr. Frasier and a younger man from the Willamette Valley had come to Lapwai to talk business with Papa. They were connected to the mission board in some way but, unlike so many of the settlers who were half-afraid of Indians, Mr. Frasier and his friend asked question after question about the Nez Perce.

The whole way from the mission, Papa had been explaining about their customs. They even stopped at an outcropping of rock so Papa could show them some of the prehistoric Nez Perce petroglyphs. The figures had been deeply etched into the stone. Eliza used to trace the drawings with her finger but Papa reminded her to look with her eyes, not with her hands. He said they must respect the ancient art just like in museum exhibits back in the States.

"Why the name Nez Perce?" Mr. Frasier asked.

Eliza knew the answer to that but she didn't dare interrupt. Instead, she looked to see if she could spot Noah in the village. She couldn't wait to show him how she had already trained Ayi to do a curvet. All she had to do was gently pull up on the reins and press her legs against the pony's sides, and Ayi leapt into the air, kicking up her hind legs just before the forelegs set down. They had practiced it over and over.

Her father answered Mr. Frasier. "It means 'pierced noses' in French. It was probably first given to them by French trappers but it's a misnomer because the Nez Perce never pierced their noses." Papa laughed as if it were a joke. "Eliza, tell them the tribe's real name."

At the mention of her name, Eliza snapped back to attention. She knew the name Nez Perce called themselves. "Numiipuu," she said proudly.

"What does that mean?" one of the men asked.

Eliza was surprised they wouldn't know. "It's the same for almost every native tribe no matter what the word is in their language. It always means 'the people.'"

The younger man cocked his head. "You mean the word Arapaho means 'the people'? Delaware?" He shook his head a little as if trying to think of other Indian names. "How very singular."

Papa answered. "Those names were given to the Indians by the white settlers and they mean various things—often not very flattering. But in each case the tribes already had their own name. The Delawares called themselves *Lenape*, which does indeed mean 'the people.'" He started to lead his horse down toward the village. "The same with the Arapaho. The word Arapaho means traders but it was given to them by outsiders. They call themselves *Hinonoeino*."

"And it means 'our people.'" Eliza laughed and nudged Ayi to get her moving.

The Spaldings enjoyed visitors who respected the ways of the Nez Perce. Too many settlers and travelers fretted about the stories of attacks and killings. They lumped all the Indians together—the outlaw bands, the warring tribes, and the gentle tribes—and spoke of them as savages or heathen. Some of their traditions may have seemed that way when you first observed them but, as Mama said, things were far less complicated and far more interesting.

When he arrived, Mr. Frasier had spent hours looking at Papa's collection of Nez Perce handcrafts. Papa traded for these and often sent gifts of artwork back to the mission board in the States to help them appreciate the Nez Perce. Because the Nez Perce fascinated these men, Mr. Frasier had asked if there was any way to see a tribal ceremony or celebration. Timothy helped Rev. Spalding organize one of the favorite Nez Perce demonstrations—a sham battle.

As they rode into the village, Eliza could see that they were prepared for the exhibition. Out in the center of the open area they had heaped a huge pile of brush and deadfall. She knew it was just pretend but she had always avoided sham battles. Noah loved the excitement of these battles. He would talk about them for days.

There was something about the whoops and fighting that made her stomach ache. But when Papa asked her if she wanted to go she had said yes. Henry wanted to stay home and hold baby Amelia, but Eliza hated to give up a chance to see Noah and Matilda. Besides, Ayi loved to ride to the village. As Eliza approached the village, she hoped she hadn't made the wrong decision. It's just pretend, she kept telling herself. Just pretend.

Before they even got off their horses, she heard a series of loud war whoops coming from all around. Ayi sidestepped and Eliza put her hand on the horse's neck to reassure the nervous pony as she slid off. Noah came and led Ayi away from all the commotion. Papa and the men stayed on their horses as Nez Perce warriors mounted on excited horses came rushing in from all directions making terrifying noises. Eliza covered her ears.

Both the Indians and their horses were painted in garish colors of red, white, and black. Mostly red. It made them seem menacing. It was hard for Eliza to look past the paint and see the Nez Perce who faithfully came to Sabbath services. She tried to remember what Mama always said, that their sham battles are just like sporting events back in the States.

Those men who were to take part drew rein at the edge of the battleground. They all carried guns and began to shoot. The noise and the smell of gunpowder added to the frenzy. With each round of gunfire, several warriors would drop as if they were dead. Papa and Mr. Frasier tried to comment to each other but the noise was deafening.

The ones who fired the sham shots went over to the fallen warriors, took out a knife and . . .

Eliza turned her head. What was happening? She had just seen an Indian slice the scalp off one of his friends.

Papa leaned down. He raised his voice over the din. "It's just pretend, 'Liza. Those are not real scalps. They are made of willow leaves."

It was real enough for Eliza. Why had she agreed to come? Her stomach lurched and she turned and ran from the battleground.

Out in the meadow with the horses she found Ayi and threw her arms around the pony's neck. "Why do people have to fight?"

"Men fight because they afraid."

She turned around to see Matilda coming up behind her. "Kat'sa. I don't like the sham battle."

Matilda put her hand on Eliza's shoulder. "Remember when Matilda's chickens fluff out feathers to look big? To look fierce?" She didn't wait for an answer. "Warriors do same.

They must protect Nez Perce so they make selves look big and scary."

"They *do* look scary, *Kat'sa*."

"Most time they plenty scared. Sham battle help prepare in case of trouble."

Eliza still didn't understand. "But why can't people just get along? Why do the men have to prepare for fights?"

Kat'sa shook her head. "Matilda not know, but always so."

5

Spring Journey

April 1847
Q'oyxt'sal—Season of High Rivers

Now don't forget the dried apples." Mama had been re-minding them about things all morning long. "Mrs. Whitman will appreciate being able to bake apple pies in the spring."

Eliza, Henry, Papa, and Noah were making the trip on horseback to the Whitman mission—a trail of over a hundred miles. Eliza couldn't wait for the journey to begin. Ayi kept snorting and sidestepping, her way of showing excitement. Eliza and Noah would each ride their ponies. Henry would ride with Papa, trailing a packhorse to carry all the things they were bringing to *Wai-i-lat-pu*, the Whitman mission.

Mama usually came along but, because of the birth of tiny Amelia and caring for Martha Jane, she couldn't travel. Besides, she kept telling them, she had too much work to do at the mission. Eliza wished the whole family could go. The way Papa kept looking over at Mama, she figured he wished so as well.

Once Mama had given the last instruction and they were finally mounted, she stood at the door with the baby in arms and waved them on their way.

The trail led out alongside the Clearwater for several miles until the place where they would have to cross the river. Eliza couldn't remember a time when the wildflowers had been more abundant. Maybe it was the sun on the flowers that made the air fairly dance with color. The fragrance changed with each step Ayi took as she inadvertently crushed one plant or another. Fields of meadow buttercup, mallow, and clover were dotted with the vibrant red of Indian paintbrush and the many purple-blue shades of violets. Bees hovered above the flowers. Eliza noticed that they always seemed to prefer the yellow blossoms. Funny. She wished there were time to stop and gather flowers. Maybe on the way home they could dig some violets to replant around the house for Mama.

Noah kept urging his pony on ahead as if the pace were too slow for him. He'd ride up ahead, circle around and come back again. Eliza wasn't sure if he was showing off his riding skills or pretending he was the scout for their party.

"Are you ready to take a little swim?" Papa turned and winked at her as they came to a wide place in the river. Crossing the river in spring could be quite an adventure, but it hadn't rained in a while and, for the most part, the snowmelt had not been heavy. The river ran swift, but they had crossed it much higher and much deeper other times. It would be Eliza's first time to cross it on her own horse.

"Make sure the horses are well watered. We don't want them stopping to drink midstream. Their hooves could sink deep into the silt of the riverbed if they tarry too long in one place. It is important that they keep moving across the stream." Papa got off his horse and led it to water. "Henry, will you make sure the packhorse gets watered?"

"Sure, Papa," Henry said. He untied the packhorse and led him to the river's edge to drink alongside his father's horse.

Papa waded into the water alone with a bundle of sticks that another traveler had left by the side of the river.

"Are you going to wait for us?" Henry asked.

Papa laughed. "I'm testing for quicksand. If the sand does not yield under my feet, we're safe to cross here." He walked slowly across, the water getting deeper and deeper toward the middle. He pushed the sharp stakes into the river bottom to mark the path all the way across.

"Reverend Spalding think like Nez Perce," Noah said, smiling.

"Is it dangerous for Papa?" Eliza never took her eyes off her father.

"Not dangerous. See, he keep moving. No time for quicksand."

Papa got to the other side, cupped his hands around his mouth and yelled across. "Good place for a ford this time of year. I'm coming back. Wait." He picked up a bundle of sharp sticks left on that side of the river and carried them back across. When he got back to the other side he dropped the sticks. "We'll leave these sticks here for the next travelers and gather up the ones we used in the ford as we move across and leave them on that side of the river."

"How will they find them?" Henry asked.

"This good place to cross river," Noah said. "Look upriver. Look downriver. Steep banks. Slippery edges. See path worn in grasses here? This best place to cross river. Wise traveler read sign."

"Noah, do you want to lead out?" Papa knew Noah had crossed many a river, as had his pony.

Noah puffed out his chest and turned to Eliza. "Don't be frighten. I teach Ayi to cross river before she come to you."

"I'm not frightened." Boys! Eliza mounted Ayi and patted her neck to reassure her.

"If something happens and you do fall off, grab onto one of the roots or branches in the stream and don't let go. I'll be coming up behind you." Papa tied the packhorse and mounted, pulling Henry up behind him.

Noah took his pony down the bank and into the river. He pressed his knees into the horse's side and urged him on, turning to call back to her. "Follow, Eliza. Come in. Ayi will follow my pony."

Eliza urged Ayi forward. She may have felt uncertain, but Ayi seemed eager to follow. Papa and Henry brought up the rear. Eliza looked back and saw him pull out a stake as he passed.

Henry kept calling out "Gee-up" as they crossed. Eliza figured he must be pretending they were part of a wagon train on the Oregon Trail. They'd heard many a story from their mother about the journey west.

When they reached the other side, Papa laid down the stakes. "Let's dry off in the sun while we have some dinner."

"I make fire," Noah offered.

The horses were happy to graze on the rich spring grasses. Eliza took out the bundle of food Mama had packed. She handed each of them a buttered baking powder biscuit filled with a thick slice of cold bacon and an apple turnover. Farther along the trail they would cook their own food, but so close to home, they could still eat Mama's cooking. Once the fire got going, Papa put the pot on a stone in the flames to boil some coffee.

Noah and Henry took off to explore but Eliza stayed with her father, enjoying the scent of coffee brewing.

"When you go to the mission for school, you'll make this trip every fall and come home in late spring." Papa handed his cup to Eliza so she could fill it with coffee.

Eliza froze, the pot of coffee still in her hand. "I heard you and Mama say something about the mission school but why do I have to leave Lapwai? Mama can still teach me."

"Pour the coffee, 'Liza, before you burn your hand." Papa held his cup steady as she poured. "Your mother and I think it important for you to study with other girls your age. Mrs.

Whitman spends much of her day teaching. It will be almost like school back in the States."

The rest of that six-day trip—two days each way and a two-day stay at the mission—Eliza refused to even think about living at the Whitman mission. She kept to herself the whole time they visited *Wai-i-lat-pu*, politely answering questions when asked but wishing she were invisible. She never once looked in the classroom.

It bothered her that Mrs. Whitman made Noah sleep outside. The Cayuse who lived around the mission seemed friendly enough but Eliza couldn't help thinking about those angry Cayuse braves they'd seen near the lodgepole pines at Lapwai. Would Noah, a Nez Perce, be safe outside all night long? Noah laughed at her worries. "I will be fine sleeping near the horses. They will alert to trouble brewing."

Eliza longed to climb onto Ayi and ride over the meadows back to Lapwai.

6

Camas Prairie

Late Summer 1847
Taya'al—Season of Hot Days

Eliza woke long before the sun began to shine. She stretched and heard the rustle of her tule mat instead of the sounds of her bed at home. Last night she had slept in the village, in Matilda's teepee. Today she would go with Matilda and some of the other village women to gather her favorite Nez Perce food, camas.

Mama had encouraged her to go, not that Eliza needed much encouraging. "Matilda is one of our dearest friends. She's getting up in years and can use your help digging camas. You have young knees."

Eliza stretched out her toes and raised her arms out as far as they could reach. She bent her legs and looked at her knees, wondering what kind of workout they would get on the Camas Prairie.

"*Tats meywi, Miya.*" Matilda often called her *miya*—child. It was a sweet word, and even though Eliza was halfway grown, she didn't mind at all. "The sun come up soon and must not find us in village. We eat on our long walk. *Éehe?*"

Eliza jumped up and pulled on her clothes. She wore an apron over her dress so that she could pull it up to fill with camas since she didn't own a camas bag like Matilda. She had left Ayi at home because they would walk to Matilda's camas meadows. In the late spring, the fields had been so full of blue and violet camas bloom that, as the wind blew across the tall flower stalks, it almost looked like waves of water. But it was not the flowers they would collect. They'd dig up the bulbs, which were almost like onions. The bulb was the edible part; of course, not without much preparation because the raw camas caused a terrible digestive flux. The work that came after the digging was why Eliza and Matilda packed food, mats, shelter, and supplies for several days.

"Why do the men not come along to help, *Kat'sa?*"

Matilda laughed. "Food, women's work. Men tend horses. Elders talk." Matilda stopped smiling. "Many problems."

Problems? Eliza frowned. She knew that girls must never ask about the elders' work. Perhaps they were deciding where the tribe resettled for winter after buffalo season. Or was it the rumblings of unrest with the Cayuse? She shivered at the thought. Settlers often talked about their fears of Indian aggression but Eliza knew the Nez Perce were their friends and loved Jesus, just like she did. At least most of them. But she didn't know much about the Cayuse. Dr. and Mrs. Whitman served the Cayuse at *Wai-i-lat-pu.*

As they walked, different women of the tribe broke off to go to their own camas meadows. Every meadow was worked by the woman who had inherited it from her ancestors. Each family respected the unmarked boundaries of their plots. Matilda's was much farther along the trail, perhaps the farthest one of all, but she confided to Eliza that her mother and many grandmothers had chosen her prairie long before any of the others. It was still the best meadow of all.

"See up there?" Matilda asked as they stopped to rest, pointing at a hill in the distance. "Coyote's Fishnet."

"Coyote's Fishnet?" Eliza was confused. "I don't see any coyotes, it's too far."

"*Nimiipuu* story, *Miya.*" Matilda said. Eliza scooted close to her. She loved to hear their ancient Coyote tales. "Long ago, *Iceye'ye*—Coyote—fished Clearwater River with big net. Quiet. Good fishing." She paused. "Then he hear branches break, water slosh. Black bear come." She inhaled and shook her head as if this were a problem. "Bear smile at *Iceye'ye* and ask why he not go with tribe to buffalo country to get food for winter. Everyone know, autumn come, people go. *Iceye'ye* go."

Matilda paused before she went on. Eliza knew not to rush her.

"*Iceye'ye* angry. He forget to go get buffalo for winter.

Shamed. Angry. He throw fishnet onto hill on south side of Clearwater and grab Black Bear by neck. He yell at Black Bear for interrupting him and throw him onto hill on north side of river. Then *Iceye'ye* leave for buffalo country."

Eliza looked up at the hill and could see the net and the black bear if she squinted her eyes. "That's a good story, *Kat'sa.*"

• • •

When they finally arrived at Matilda's meadow, it was close to twilight. They wouldn't begin digging until morning.

"Shall I set up the shelter?" It was not a teepee, but more like a lean-to with several tule mats thrown over it. Because the weather was mild, they had no need for a fire inside. The teepee back in the village had an opening in the peak for smoke to escape, but for these few days, they didn't need the inside fire. An outside fire would be fine.

"*Éehe.*" Matilda nodded as she laid out the tools they would use for digging camas. She had the old hoe she had used since she was a girl. Eliza had brought a small hand hoe from home. There was a knife for separating bulbs and a sack for collecting the harvest. With all the tools laid out, Matilda started the fire to begin cooking their supper.

Eliza took out her journal. She had tucked it in her pack, hoping she'd have time to note details of her time with Matilda. "I wish I had the right words to describe the color of the flowers and grasses."

Matilda laughed. "*Éehe*, I search words in your language much."

"Yes, just like I do in Nez Perce. I know I sometimes sound like a baby when I talk your language. Actually, your little ones chatter away without ever having to pause to reach for a word."

"True of first language. Natural." Matilda paused as she often did. She never apologized for taking time to frame her thoughts. "*Nimiipuu* language not use helper words."

"Words like 'the,' right? Mama says that we call those words 'articles' in English grammar." Eliza was proud of what she had learned from her father while translating. Matilda's English sounded choppy to English speakers but it was because she translated Nez Perce words directly into English in her mind and just left out the words that didn't occur in Nez Perce.

"I know I speak English rough. Not good at adding words make language flow like river. I still learn."

And Eliza knew she would continue to learn. Matilda was the wisest Nez Perce she knew. Even the elders listened to her. Papa said no one should ever make judgments about a man's intelligence by how he communicated in a second language. Or how he communicated at all. Some of the wisest people were listeners. Mostly silent.

Eliza wished she could communicate this in her journal, but it was complicated. She wrote it down the best she could and ended with another Bible verse she had memorized last year. *"My little children, let us not love in word, neither in tongue; but in deed and in truth."* 1 John 3:18.

The next morning they awakened before the sun. Eliza went down to the stream to wash and get water. On her way back to camp, she saw two women digging camas just beyond the rise. "*Kat'sa*, isn't this your ancestral camas plot?" she asked as soon as she came up close to the fire.

"*Éehe, Miya*, yes."

"Then why are those Cayuse women digging camas over there?"

Matilda looked up, her brow wrinkling. "Come. We talk."

They walked over to where the women were digging. They already had a pile of camas bulbs on a cloth on the ground. Matilda spoke in Nez Perce but it was close enough to the Cayuse language that they could understand each other. Their gestures were angry and the younger one kept pointing—almost jabbing—with her finger toward Eliza.

Eliza understood that they were angry because white settlers had taken their camas plots. They blamed Matilda and her tribe for inviting the *Su-i-yap-po* to come to their tribal lands.

As they continued to talk and gesture, Eliza looked up to the sharp rise toward the north and saw two Cayuse warriors on their horses, keeping watch over the women. They wore the paint of battle. Eliza caught her breath and then had to remind herself to breathe again. She missed what Matilda and the women said.

As they walked back to camp, Eliza asked, "Did you see those Cayuse on the sharp rise?"

"*Éehe.*"

"What does it mean, *Kat'sa*?"

"Cayuse angry. Frightened. Much change."

"Are they angry at my family?" Eliza couldn't forget that finger jabbing.

"Cayuse not understand. Some Cayuse, not all Cayuse. Settlers build on Cayuse lands."

Eliza understood the problem. The settlers came, wagon train after wagon train, and most moved on toward the Whitman mission where they saw what looked like rich, open land, free for the taking. If they made it that far, they simply fenced off the fertile land and called it their own. They didn't understand that these were tribal lands, belonging to the Cayuse for centuries. It might look like empty land but Papa said it took miles and miles of land to support a tribe because they hunted and gathered their food. They never wanted to take too much game from one area so they traveled far each year to hunt. The same with gathering camas and other plants. They need enough land to take what they needed and still leave plenty to grow for the next season.

"What did you decide?" Eliza asked.

"Cayuse women dig camas until Chinook salmon return. Next year find new field." Matilda was silent for a time. "Cayuse elders, *Nimiipuu* must talk." Matilda picked up her hoe and her sharp pointed stick. "Come, *Miya*. Time to work."

She first showed how to tell the true camas from the poisonous death camas, but over the years, she had completely removed every poisonous bulb she came across in her field.

Today they only found one straggly one, near the edge. She pulled it up and, using her hoe, chopped it into tiny pieces.

The first step in harvesting was to carefully remove the turf. They slid their hoes under the grass and lifted a patch, setting it aside. The sun grew warm as they worked, and Eliza was glad she'd carried plenty of water from the stream for drinking. It was still cool and tasted sweet.

Once the grass was removed they took the pointed sticks and dug out the largest camas bulbs, carefully separating the clumps of side bulbs and replanting them. They also left the slender bulbs for next season. "It ensures enough camas for the future, right, *Kat'sa*?"

"As long as *Nimiipuu* fields remain," she said as she carefully replaced the turf, moving on to a new section.

Every time Eliza looked up, she could see the two warriors, seated on their horses, still as statues. She shivered in spite of the warm sun. She thought of Lapwai and longed to talk to her mother about the way things seemed to be changing.

When they reckoned they had dug enough bulbs to last for the year, they dug a huge pit, lined it with grass, and started a fire. Once the wood had burned to red coals, they covered them with camas leaves and piled the bulbs on top. They covered the smoking pit with a tule mat.

The sun set as they finished. "Camas cook all night, all day, all night."

"That's a long time," Eliza said. Thirty-six hours.

"Long time for sweet, like Lapwai sugar." Matilda explained.

They walked back to the camp and set about making a fire and enjoying fry bread, berries, and pemmican for dinner. "Tomorrow, we make paints for *Miya* journal."

"For me?" Eliza clapped her hands. It was just like Matilda to have been planning how she could fulfill Eliza's longing to capture the color of the land.

The next day, while the camas cooked in the pit, they dug up clay by the side of the stream and kneaded it until it was smooth and pliable. Matilda showed Eliza how to make little clay pots and lids for the paints they would make. Pulling up the tule mat that covered the pit, Matilda carefully put the tiny pots into the smoking pit, right along with the baking camas.

Matilda guided her to collect berries and different colors of clay—some by the stream's edge, others in the dry cracked ground. Eliza never noticed how many different, rich colors of earth could be found. They collected some of the charcoal near the pit and even the hulls of walnuts they'd brought from Lapwai. They ground each of these, adding buffalo grease Matilda brought for cooking. Eliza was surprised by the colors that developed. When the little pots were finally fired, they would put each color into its pot.

Matilda took a stubby branch and begin to carve and smooth it. "Find squirrel tail, *Miya*," she directed.

Yuck. Eliza didn't like this part. Looking for a dead squirrel. She wished Noah or Henry were here. When she finally found one, she took a broad leaf and wrapped it around the carcass so she wouldn't have to touch it or see it.

She couldn't help but admire the way Matilda took the fine end of that tail and fashioned it into a paintbrush, setting it into a deep hole in the end of the handle she'd been carving. She secured it with sinew around the bristles and through tiny notches in the wood. Mama had once said that the finest European painters prized the Nez Perce squirrel tail brushes.

The next morning they opened the pit. Matilda took out the pots with a potholder fashioned out of leather. After they cooled, Eliza set about putting her paints in their pots. She felt like a real artist with her rainbow of paints and a real squirrel tail brush. She ran over to Matilda, who was leaning over the pit, carefully removing the burned grasses one layer at a time, and said, "Thank you, *Kat'sa,* for my paints and brush. I will treasure them forever."

Matilda stood up and hugged her. Eliza knew change was coming and they may never share harvest again. Soon she and Matilda would head back to the village with their harvest of camas. Eliza would then go back to Lapwai, but only for a fortnight or so when she would travel to the Whitman mission for school. She didn't want to think about it—about all the goodbyes, her friends, her family, and even Ayi.

For now, it was enough to enjoy the last bit of summer on the camas prairie.

7

The Severe Schoolroom

September 1847
Piq'unmayq'al—Season of Chinook Salmon Return

Eliza stood just outside the Whitman mission door, waving at her father as he rode away on his horse, Tashe. Riding next to him was Dr. Whitman with his medical bag tied securely to the pommel of his saddle. They planned to head over to Umatilla to help with a strange sickness reported to have overtaken the people there. It would be a long day's ride and hard days helping with the sick Indian people when they arrived. Papa promised to come back to *Wai-i-lat-pu* to say goodbye to Eliza before he began his journey back to Lapwai.

As the two men turned onto the road, Eliza felt alone. Not that there weren't seventy or so people at the mission, counting all the emigrants and the other children there for school, but she missed Ayi and her mother, her brother, and her sisters. She hadn't wanted to come here to school. Her mother taught her from the time she could first remember and Mama was a patient, interesting teacher, but both her parents thought coming to the Whitman school was a great chance to learn with other children and make new friends.

Eliza moved away from the front door and rounded the outside of the whitewashed adobe building to the school-room door. All of the rooms in the large mission house were connected. It made one large building on the outside, but you couldn't move from room to room through doorways or hall-ways once past the main lodgings. You entered the schoolroom, the dormitory, and the washrooms through outside doors.

Most one-room schools, back in the States, had two doors, one for the girls and one for the boys, according to Eliza's mother, but the Whitman school was too small for that. Mrs. Whitman thought it made more sense to divide the students by age and ability. Those she called the "Littles" were seated up front. They were the students who were mostly six, seven, or eight. The "Middles," which included Eliza, who was now ten years old, sat in the middle of the room. They were nine, ten, and eleven. In the back of the room sat the "Uppers," who were twelve and thirteen. Those who were older sat in chairs around the outside walls. Their job was to continue their own education in the evenings through reading, memorization, and discussion. During the morning, they helped teach the Littles and sometimes the Middles. In the afternoons, they learned homesteading skills. The boys helped in the gristmill or on the farm, the butchery, or the carpenter shop. The girls helped in the kitchen and with the infants.

At the time Eliza arrived, there were about seventy emigrants—families who had been following the Oregon Trail out west and decided to stay at the mission for the winter rather than travel on to their homesteads.

Eliza had made friends with all the Middle girls. There was Nancy Osborne, Phebe Saunders, Gertrude Hall, Helen Meek, and Elizabeth Sager, but Elizabeth and Helen became her best friends. Elizabeth and her six brothers and sisters were orphans, taken in by Dr. and Mrs. Whitman. Their mother and father had died on the trail out to the west. Eliza couldn't imagine living without her mother and father. The thought made her breath catch in her throat.

Elizabeth was small for her age, probably because food had been scarce for much of her life before coming to *Wai-i-lat-pu*, but she had skin the color of the china doll that was displayed with a wreath of dried field flowers high on a shelf. Eliza knew she was considered "a beauty," because Mrs. Whitman often smiled at her and said, "Pretty is as pretty does."

Helen Meek had come to live with the Whitmans when she was little. Her mother, who Helen said was a Nez Perce, died when Helen was just a baby. She had her mother's dark skin and hair. "My father is a great trapper, guide, and mountain man," she told the class while they played outside at recess.

"He is not," Edwin said. "How is it we've never seen him?"

Helen looked like she might cry. Mary Ann Bridger, one of

the Uppers, came over and put her arm around Helen. "Joseph Lafayette Meek is indeed an important man," she said with a sniff. "He is known by every chief in the Northwest and often works for the Hudson's Bay Company. He's a legislator for the Oregon Provisional Government," she finished with a flip of her braid.

Eliza smiled at the way Mary Ann said his three names with such a flourish.

"If he's so important, why is Helen a half-breed?" Edwin wanted to know.

Eliza held her breath. At her home they never talked about people that way. The schoolmaster, Mr. Saunders, was standing nearby. Surely he had heard.

"Helen's mother was a Nez Perce princess," Mary Ann said. "My father and Helen's are friends. Did you know that Helen's father is a cousin to President Polk's wife back in the States?"

Eliza knew about President Polk from reading newspapers settlers had left at Lapwai. She looked at Helen with new interest. What a fascinating group of students in this little classroom, all making history together.

Mary Ann was not finished. "And in case you want to call *me* names, Edwin Smith, *my* mother was Cora, daughter of Insala, chief of the Flathead nation. A chief is like your president. And my father is Jim Bridger, and he's also a famous trapper. He built the trading post now called Fort Bridger. My father can speak French, English, and all the western native languages." She turned on her heel, dismissing Edwin, to go join the Uppers a little ways apart.

Mr. Saunders caught her arm. "Do you remember that poem we learned about humility, Miss Bridger? I'd like you to rejoin the class by pulling your chair into the corner for the rest of the morning."

Edwin smiled. Apparently Mr. Saunders didn't mind name calling if it was aimed at girls. Or was it because of Mary Ann's and Helen's mothers?

After midday dinner, served in what was once called the Indian Room, the Middles cleared the tables and swept the floor. The Uppers would do the dishes before they came back to the schoolroom.

Afternoons were much better than mornings. In the morning they began with Bible. Mrs. Whitman insisted that every student memorize eleven verses a week, so those were assigned and practiced all week and recited on Saturday morning. School went from Monday morning to Saturday noon. After Bible, they had Latin, arithmetic, followed by arithmetic drills, then grammar, reading, and elocution—which was the practice of clear speaking or, as Mr. Saunders told them in his measured tone, "It teaches you to speak expressively, with clarity, distinct pronunciation, and articulation." The trouble with that was that by the time they got to elocution it was almost time for dinner. How could she possibly be expected to read Percy Shelley's *To a Skylark* with a watering mouth?

Hail to thee, blithe Spirit!
Bird thou never wert,
That from Heaven, or near it,

Pourest thy full heart
In profuse strains of unpremeditated art.

It wasn't that Eliza wasn't interested in elocution. Her father had the most refined voice she had ever heard. When he read the Bible, she could listen forever. But today, when the big girls were braising pork, mashing potatoes, and baking apple pies, before she even got to "blithe spirit," she knew she would earn that embarrassing ruler snap on her cheek with Mr. Saunders muttering, "Enunciate, girl."

But afternoons were pure joy. Miss Bewley, who traveled from the States with her brother, taught what she called the refined arts to the girls—those skills Eliza had never quite mastered back in Lapwai. Without the distractions of Ayi, Noah, and the printing press, she found she wasn't quite as hopeless as she'd been led to believe. She, Helen, and Elizabeth were working on embroidered samplers. They were to complete them by mid-October and surprise Mrs. Whitman with the work of their hands, as Miss Bewley called it. Gertrude, Phebe, and Nancy were practicing watercolors. When they were done, they would switch and Eliza would try her hand at painting with watercolors. It reminded her of the paints she and Matilda had made out on the camas prairie. She was glad she had brought them with her. She wished she could find time to write in her journal.

At the end of the day came lessons in comportment— good manners. They studied proper table settings using Mrs. Whitman's good china and silver. They practiced walking and sitting like a lady. Eliza even mastered a proper curtsy.

"Eliza," whispered Helen, "I can't stop thinking of how Mrs. Whitman called Nez Perce traditions strange." She giggled. "If my mother's people saw me walking around the classroom with a book on my head, they'd tease me forever."

Eliza laughed. Helen was right. Now that she was immersed in the culture of white folk, for the mission had no Cayuse visitors to speak of, she felt as if she had entered a different world.

That's what struck her as so strange. At Lapwai, the Nez Perce were as much a part of their lives at the mission as any emigrants or the Spaldings themselves. The native women walked right into Mama's kitchen, bringing gifts of food or borrowing some apples or vegetables. The schoolroom back home at Lapwai served the Nez Perce of all ages, teaching them their own written language so they could read. The schoolroom here at *Wai-i-lat-pu* was for white settlers' children and the children fostered by the Whitman family.

The Cayuse had never been allowed into the Whitman home, except for the room they called the Indian Room, which was reached by an outside door or Dr. Whitman's surgery. But since Mrs. Whitman had decided to start the school, the Indian Room was used for a dining room and the Cayuse were no longer welcome.

This bothered Eliza. She'd watched young Cayuse men hovering around the door, muttering to each other. They didn't know she could speak and understand their language.

She was the only one at Whitman mission aside from the doctor who could.

"Watch. These white men come hungry. See? Dr. Whitman freely gives food to the white men. But when Cayuse come hungry, Dr. Whitman sells a small bit of food to us—not gives, but sells. He makes us work for every morsel of food or piece of meat that comes from the land. Our tribal land." The young brave stabbed his tomahawk into a tree stump near the door and spit on the ground.

"The white people came, first one family, then two families, but now a flood of families. At first we welcomed them. We gave the Whitmans land to use. Now they tell us to 'get off our land.'" The man rocked back and forth in anger. "This is the land the Great God gave us to protect. Cayuse land. We did not protect it. We foolishly loaned it to Dr. Whitman."

The first man spoke again. "Joe Lewis speaks about the white people coming this *Taya'al*—summer. He says four thousand more will come. There will be no room for Cayuse."

Eliza quietly slipped away. She wished Papa were here so she could tell him. Joe Lewis was a bad man. She'd heard Papa say that the Hudson's Bay Company fired him because he started trouble wherever he went. Now he was with the Cayuse stirring up trouble. She knew they called Mr. Lewis a half-breed—that word Papa hated. He was half Delaware Indian and half French-American. He'd been a trapper and a vagabond. Joe Lewis was stirring the pot again and there was no telling what evil would come of it.

She had never felt so homesick in her life. She remem-bered her mother saying in times of worry, "Don't fear, little Eliza, this world is not our final home." She knew what her mother meant but as she looked over all the faces here at the Whitman mission, she knew that this particular world—*Wai-i-lat-pu*—was certainly not her home. As she crawled into her bunk that night, she thought of Matilda and Timothy, of Noah and Ayi, of her brother and sisters and mostly of her mother and father. She reached for the handkerchief she had tucked into the sleeve of her nightgown.

• • •

The next morning she felt more composed. She sensed that trouble was surrounding them but as she prayed last night, she felt a calm. No matter what happened, God never left her.

After Bible studies that morning, it was time for Latin. Mr. Saunders looked at Helen. "Miss Meek, can you tell me how many verb tenses there are in Latin?"

Helen stood up by the side of her desk and in her quiet voice answered, "There are six verb tenses in Latin, sir."

"Correct." Then he looked straight at Eliza. "Miss Spalding, are you ready to name the six Latin verb tenses?"

"Yes, sir." She named them, slowly, in order. "Present. Im-perfect. Future. Perfect. Pluperfect. Future perfect."

"Correct." He started to turn to someone else, but Eliza continued to stand. The teacher asked, "Did you have some-thing else to say, Miss Spalding?"

The eyes of each student in the room locked on Eliza.

"Sir, you told us in the beginning of this term that Latin was a dead language. If that is so, why are we not learning a living language, like Cayuse, so we could communicate with the people around us?" Eliza could feel her hands shaking but she believed it was an important question.

"You are impertinent, Miss Spalding," he sputtered. "Mrs. Whitman wants to give you a classical education. Latin is part of that education so you can read the classics in the original language." His face grew red. "And you ask why we should not learn the language of savages! Of heathen!"

He was shouting now. "Tell me how many important works of literature are written in Cayuse? How many books of mathematics can you find in that language? What in the world would be the purpose of learning gibberish?"

"It would allow us to tell the Cayuse people about Jesus," she answered, twisting the bottom of her apron.

"Get out of my classroom, this minute," he said, stabbing his finger toward the door. "Go to your dormitory and spend the rest of the day alone. You may read your Bible, write in your journal, and focus on schoolwork. Tomorrow, I expect an apology before the entire class."

Eliza did as she was told, but she knew an apology would be difficult. What was not difficult was having a day to be alone with her Bible and journal. She got a little cup of water from the washroom for her paintbrush and cleaning her pen nib. She sat on the floor between the end of the bunk and the wall and spread out her Bible, her journal, her pen, ink, paints, and her sampler.

September 15, 1847

I find little time to be alone here at the Whitman mission. There are people everywhere, coming and going. Emigrants, just stopping with the hope of getting provisions, little children too young to go to school, who come with their mothers from the emigrant house to the big house. The mothers help in the kitchen while the toddlers tumble all over, getting into things. It makes me miss my little sisters, Martha Jane and baby Amelia.

I spent some time reading in my Bible this morning and read a passage I want to read again in Nez Perce. It was 1 Peter 5:10. It read, "But the God of all grace, who hath called us unto his eternal glory by Christ Jesus, after that ye have suffered a while, make you perfect, stablish, strengthen, settle you."

It reminds me again what Mama always says; this world is not my home. We may suffer a while but that is what will eventually perfect us, establish us, strengthen us, and finally settle us. I don't look forward to the suffering but I will work to find joy here in spite of discomfort.

As I look out the window at the fields of gentle rye grass, swaying in the breeze, that is what I'll paint today here in my journal. I wish I could catch the sound and the smell with my paintbrush. It is a gift from God and it makes me happy.

After she finished in her journal, she put away her ink and paints and went to the washroom to wash out the cup. She slipped back into the dormitory and took out her linen sampler and her spools of floss. Before she even realized her belly was rumbling, her friend Elizabeth came in and pulled something wrapped in a piece of cloth from her apron pocket. She unwrapped it and Eliza saw half an apple and a small piece of ham on a half slice of bread. "I couldn't eat it all," she fibbed, hugging Eliza.

"You are such a dear friend. What would I do without you and Helen?"

"Was it awful, sitting in here all morning long?"

Eliza laughed. "You remember what Joseph said to his brothers in Egypt? I thought the same thing this morning. What Mr. Saunders meant for evil, God meant for good." She scrunched up her nose. "Well, in truth, the evil may have been in my attitude toward a teacher, but he meant it for punishment and yet it was just what I needed. I spent time with the Lord, in His Word, and decided to seek the good in the middle of any suffering."

Elizabeth smiled. "Have you worked on your apology?"

"No, but I will have no trouble apologizing for questioning him about what is important to learn and I will apply myself studiously to Latin."

"Not me, but I need to go to class. I don't want to be late."

"Thanks for sharing your food with me." Eliza patted her stomach.

8

Measles

October 1847
Hoplal—Season of Tamarack Turns Yellow

Presentation Day fell on Saturday, October 16. This was Mrs. Whitman's way of seeing what her students had accomplished so far. Each student had to recite the Bible verses memorized over the last month—all fifty of them. Eliza wasn't too worried about that; she had been repeating them every day for more than a week. By the time all twenty-one students had repeated the verses it was noon, time for dinner, but the presentations would continue all day, not just the regular half day of school as on other Saturdays.

The big girls, Helen Saunders, Susan, and Mary, set the head table with Mrs. Whitman's blue willow china and silverware, treasured and brought to the mission in a trunk from her home in Prattsburgh, New York. Before the food was served,

Mrs. Whitman and Miss Bewley judged the correctness of the table setting. Besides the china, there were two spoons at each setting, two forks, a table knife, and a butter knife. All needed to be in their proper place. Once it was deemed they had done it correctly, the girls were sent to serve the first course, since they were practicing what Mrs. Whitman called *Service a la Russe.* They had planned and cooked each course as their presentation.

At the head table sat Dr. and Mrs. Whitman, Miss Bewley, and Mr. Saunders. Dr. Whitman had returned from Umatilla a fortnight ago without Papa. He'd explained that there was much sickness there and that her father had stayed to help care for the sick, but he would still stop at *Wai-i-lat-pu* to greet her before going home.

Eliza was glad she and the other students sat at their regular places, with everyday dishes and utensils. She knew the students were to receive comportment marks for their table manners, but with all the silver at the head table, she would never have stood a chance of knowing which fork was for what.

Mary carried in a beautiful soup tureen and gently set it down before Mrs. Whitman, bobbing a curtsy before stepping back.

Dr. Whitman prayed and then Mrs. Whitman lifted the lid of the tureen and inhaled the scent of the soup. "Nice choice, Mary. A savory squash soup is always welcome in autumn."

Top marks for Mary, Eliza guessed.

When they had finished the soup and the girls had cleared

the bowls, Helen Saunders—they always used both her first and last names, Helen and Saunders, so as not to confuse her with Helen Meek—carried in the serving dishes of the main course.

She set a platter of fall root vegetables roasted in the oven.

"Again, a perfect choice for a cold day. I'm glad to see you roasted onions with the squashes and potatoes. Adding beets gave this dish a nice colorful presentation."

Eliza heard some noise outside and saw four or five young Cayuse men peering in the window.

"Just ignore our uninvited guests, children," Mrs. Whitman said. "Perhaps they will benefit from seeing what a civilized dinner looks like."

"Narcissa!" Dr. Whitman frowned. "Don't forget, this is the Indian Room from which they've been banished, now that you've started your school." He rarely used Mrs. Whitman's first name in front of the students, so Eliza guessed that he didn't approve.

Rather than respond, Mrs. Whitman pursed her lips and served some of the vegetables to each one at the head table and had Helen Saunders pass the plate on to the students.

John and Francis Sager brought in a huge platter of roast beef and set it in front of the doctor with the carving knife. "We roasted the beef outdoors in the clay oven. We started the fire hot so that the outside of the roast would get dark and seal in the juice just like Miss Bewley said." John seemed uncomfortable in this role of chef. At least they could cook outdoors so it seemed more manly than donning an apron and cooking in the kitchen. His brother Francis added, "We let the roast rest for half of an hour."

The doctor carved the roast and lay aside end pieces which were well done and served each person at the head table juicy center slices. John and Francis carried the heavy platter to the student tables. Francis held the platter while John served each student his or her preferred slice.

"Very nice, gentlemen," Mrs. Whitman said when they had finished. "The roast was done to a turn and the polite manner in which you served the meat added to our enjoyment."

Eliza couldn't help but smile as John whispered in an English-like accent as they headed back to the kitchen, "How very splendid. Think I can get a job as a butler here in Oregon territory?" Mrs. Whitman did not hear, luckily for John Sager.

Finally, it was time for dessert. Susan first brought out a berry compote topped with sweet cream and placed it on the head table. She followed that with a plate of four pretty fluted Savoy sponge cakes. Helen Saunders and Mary carried plates of individual Savoy sponges to each table of students and carefully served a sponge to each student, followed by a berry compote for each table.

Mrs. Whitman served each of those at the head table, using the tongs to place a sponge on their dessert plate and then spoon the berries and cream over the top. When she finished, Susan came to stand before Mrs. Whitman.

"Very nice choice, Susan. The last of the summer berries

and a light dessert. You've learned well. If one has a heavy meal, choose a light dessert. If a light meal is served, one can offer a rich dessert."

When everyone had finished their desserts, Mrs. Whitman stood up to speak. Dr. Whitman stood up as well and excused himself to go back to the surgery.

"The three ladies and two gentlemen have comported themselves nicely. I hope you will all take time to thank them for a special meal. We will leave them to clear the table and help the kitchen women do the dishes, while we take a short break. Don't forget, Miss Bewley was taking notes on your own manners at the table and will give a short review. I will meet you in the classroom at two o'clock precisely. We will then grade your projects. Littles, bring your sewing projects, Middles, your paintings or sampler, and Uppers, your book-binding projects."

Chatter arose as they hurried out of the dining room for a short break before the second half of the day. Eliza could see a number of Cayuse standing around the doctor's surgery with hard faces, shifting from one foot to the other. Joe Lewis stood a way off. The doctor stepped out and handed a vial of medicine to each man, plus one of the folded papers that held powdered medicine to one of them.

"Come on, Eliza," Helen said. "Me and Elizabeth want to walk down to the emigrant house to hold some of the babies. We'll get back in time to get our samplers and be in our seats before two."

Eliza looked at the position of the sun in the sky. "Okay, but we can only spare a half hour, so let's run."

• • •

Seated in the classroom once again, Eliza watched while the Littles showed off their sewing projects. Byron, Alfred, and Charles had made drawstring marble bags out of cotton ticking. Miss Bewley helped them learn to make French seams so that the bags were strong and they'd never lose a marble.

Matilda, Hannah, Mary Catherine, Ann Eliza, and Sarah Sophia all made rag dolls and stuffed them by themselves, making wigs out of yarn. Each doll had a simple day dress and a nightgown. Eliza guessed they'd had a bit of help from their mothers but they were so proud of their work. Their smiles matched the little crescent moon smiles on the dolls' faces.

"Fine achievement, all of you." Mrs. Whitman beamed. This kind of work was near and dear to her heart.

Now it would be the Middles. The art presentations were first. Nancy brought her paintings and lay them on the table in front of Mrs. Whitman and Miss Bewley.

"Very nice, Nancy," Mrs. Whitman said, looking at each in turn.

"Do you notice how Nancy chose to focus on landscapes?" Miss Bewley pointed out to Mrs. Whitman. "Each girl ended up preferring a different type of subject."

"I do believe you handle the trees very well and each is nicely balanced. You can be considered proficient in watercolor."

Nancy let out a breath as if she hadn't dared to breathe the whole time.

Phebe came second. She set her paintings down and stood back.

"Why, Phebe. You've done botanical watercolors. These are pleasing."

"Th-thank you, ma'am. I l-like science best of all, so I th-thought I'd do a study of f-flowers around the m-mission and try to p-paint them accurately." She often stuttered when she was nervous.

"I think these are lovely and educational besides. Nice work."

Gertrude was last. With shaking hands, she lay out her three paintings where Phebe had picked up hers. "This shows great promise," Mrs. Whitman said as she studied the first and second paintings. One was a back view of the doctor riding off on his horse and the second was her classmate David Malin, standing by the tall rye grass. "Your ability to catch the essence of the person with just a few strokes is excellent."

She picked up the third painting, a scene of the river with one of the emigrant toddlers squatting beside it to pick flowers that grew at the edge of the water. Eliza thought it was an especially sweet painting.

Mrs. Whitman was silent. She started to speak and began to breathe heavily instead. As she sat back in her chair, Miss Bewley stood up hastily and said, "Let's take a break before we present the rest of the Middles. I'll ring the bell when it is time to gather again."

Eliza walked slowly out of the room and put her arm around

Gertrude who looked stricken. "It's a beautiful painting, Gertrude. It must have reminded Mrs. Whitman of something. Please don't fret."

Mary Ann Bridger came up to them and spoke softly. "You couldn't have known because no ever mentions it, but my father told me long before I came to the mission."

The secret. This, Eliza knew, was the answer to the secret she'd long wondered about.

"Dr. and Mrs. Whitman had a little girl, their only natural born child. She was the first white child born west of the Continental Divide. One beautiful afternoon, Mrs. Whitman sat by the river with Alice Clarissa, who was two. She'd brought a book with and was so caught up in the story she didn't notice that Alice had toddled away. When she looked up and couldn't see her little girl, she began screaming. Everyone came to search. Alice was finally found in the river, drowned."

"Oh, no." Gertrude started crying.

"My father said she grieved harder than any woman he'd ever seen. Grieved and blamed herself mercilessly. She became sad and sickly, rarely leaving her bed. She didn't start to get better until David's mother, who didn't want a baby, left him at the mission. And then Mr. Meek brought Helen. Those two began to fill a terrible void."

"What a tragedy," Eliza said. "No wonder no one wants to speak about it." And that's why I'm the second child born in the territory but the first to grow up here, Eliza thought. Alice must have been born before me.

"But don't worry, Gertrude." Mary Ann said. "Miss Bewley was with you when you painted that, wasn't she? She'll explain who the child is and how you came to paint her and that the little girl's mother was right beside her daughter but you only wanted to paint the child."

They heard the bell ring. Gertrude dabbed at her eyes with her apron and they hurried back.

When they were all seated, the room was hushed. Mrs. Whitman stood and asked Gertrude to come forward. "Forgive me, child. I must have been a little faint this afternoon. I have a favor to ask."

Eliza could tell even from that side that Gertrude, with eyes still red from crying, looked puzzled.

"May I have that painting? The one by the river? Or did you promise it to the child's mother?"

"No. I didn't promise it and yes, please, I'd be honored for you to have it."

Mrs. Whitman came around the table and hugged Gertrude. "Time for the boys to show us their handiwork."

David, John Duncan, and Edwin came forward together. Each had crafted a wooden tray with inlaid pieces of wood. John Duncan had done a checkerboard design using red cedar and white oak. The tray itself was white oak. He had also made checkers out of red cedar rounds and white oak rounds.

"Very creative, John Duncan," Mrs. Whitman said. "It is perfect for taking meals into a sickroom and then playing checkers with the invalid as the meal is finished."

Edwin's tray resembled a patchwork quilt of wood. He had even used little Xs of metal and pounded them in to look like the decorative thread stitching holding the patches together.

"What can I say, Edwin? You've done a fine job."

David was last. His tray had tiny inlaid wood pieces that he had stained in subtle colors to look like tile and he created a mosaic of the blue field lupine that was Mrs. Whitman's favorite flower. "This tray is for you, Mother."

"Thank you, David. It's beautiful and I shall treasure it. Top marks for all three of our woodworking artists." She turned to Miss Bewley. "Don't you think all the students have been exceptional so far?"

"They've worked very hard, and many of the emigrants wintering here have shared their skills and helped teach."

"Let's see the needlework next. Helen?"

Helen came to the front and held out her sampler. It was unframed because Miss Bewley said it was important to make sure the back was as neat as the front.

Miss Bewley explained that each girl was required to choose her own silk colors, stitch her name, her age, and the year and place. She must embroider the uppercase and lower case alphabet and numerals from 0–9. She could stitch a Bible verse or a saying on it. After that, it was up to her how to decorate it. Many samplers had flowers embroidered as a border, some even had their house in the center or a spreading oak. No two samplers were ever alike.

Mrs. Whitman took Helen's sampler and turned it over

to check for neatness. Then she studied the front. It had all the required points all done neatly in a pleasing indigo color. Each line of numbers and letters was set off by a double line with tiny multicolored flowers embroidered in between.

"Very neat, Helen. Very pretty and your stiches are tiny and uniform. All your knots and thread tails are hidden. Tell me about the saying you decided to embroider. 'Sloth Impoverishes.' Did you choose that because it is short?"

"No, Mother," Helen said in her thin voice. "I chose it because it is true. Sloth in our world means lazy. And that is true. If one is lazy, he will be poor. That's the simple meaning but there is a deeper meaning."

"Which is?" Mrs. Whitman leaned forward, interested.

"In the Bible sloth means being lazy about spiritual things. If we become slothful we will impoverish our spirits."

"I see. Where did you learn that truth?"

"From Father. He taught it one night in our Bible study."

"I like that you embroidered our mission there in the middle. It's a fine job. Elizabeth? Your turn."

Elizabeth brought hers up and handed it to Mrs. Whitman who studied it intently.

"Good work. Fine, even stitches. Pretty color in that deep rose. I like the verse you chose. 'Remember Thy Creator.' I think you chose a nice decoration in that spreading oak tree with the birds on each side." Mrs. Whitman smiled at Elizabeth. "Eliza?"

Eliza lay her sampler out on the table.

Mrs. Whitman glanced at the sampler and raised her eyes to

Eliza. "Please explain this to me." This time she did not smile.

"I used a deep blue for the alphabet, numbers, my name, age, and *Wai-i-lat-pu*. I think my stitches are small and even." She looked up at Mrs. Whitman. Suddenly she felt unsure of her work.

"That's not what concerns me. Please explain the whole sampler to me."

"Miss Bewley had a book with pictures of samplers and we saw that there were several kinds including pictorial or figural. I chose to stitch two figures facing each other with outstretched hands, one earth-colored and one pale-colored. That went along with my verse, 'Blessed are the peacemakers.' For the border I used beads given to me by my Nez Perce *Kat'sa* in a design I've seen her work." Eliza didn't want to make excuses. She liked the way her sampler looked. It represented her—one foot in the white man's world, one foot with the Nez Perce. But she was concerned by the disappointment clearly written on Mrs. Whitman's face.

"I did tell them it was up to them to decide how to decorate their samplers." Miss Bewley sounded uncertain.

"The sampler is an established New England tradition, Eliza Spalding. There are parameters and you have crossed them. I want you to put that sampler away and start over. I want to see a traditional sampler, not some fanciful experiment."

Eliza went back to her seat, folded her sampler to fit in the soft buffalo hide bag Matilda had given her for her birthday. She remembered what her *Kat'sa* had said when she gave her the beads. "Your mother wishes you to learn needlework like white women learn, but Matilda thinks you can include *Nimiipuu* designs in needlework."

She couldn't wait to show Matilda her sampler. She, at least, would be proud of Eliza.

Mrs. Whitman shook her head, as if to try to forget what she had just seen. "Last, we have the Uppers who learned bookbindery. Each one of you has been given a different piece of leather, tanned for us by the men working in the butchery. You were to scrape and work the leather until it was buttery soft and bind four old books whose covers were missing."

The four older students came forward and lay their books on the table. They stood quietly while Mrs. Whitman went over the books, looking at how tight the leather stretched over the boards, how strongly the cords on the spine stood out, and the quality of the endpapers. "Having a settler who studied traditional bookbinding back in the States is a blessing indeed. Now will each one of you tell us one part of the—"

Mary Ann Bridger silently slipped to the floor, hitting her head on a desk as she went down. Catherine immediately went to her, looking up at Mrs. Whitman. "She's been feeling unwell, but she didn't want to miss Presentation Day."

"Lorinda, I mean Miss Bewley, get the doctor."

Dr. Whitman came rushing in, took one quick look at Mary Ann and then carefully moved her to a place on the floor where he could see her more clearly. "Narcissa, get me some cool water and soft rags. This is what I have been fearing."

"What have you been fearing?" Mrs. Whitman looked troubled.

"The Cayuse have been struck with a particularly virulent strain of measles. Many have died. Because you have kept such a separation from the natives, I hoped it wouldn't strike the mission, but it has." He looked up and seemed to notice, for the first time, all the students still in the room.

"Children," he said, "leave at once and go back to the dormitory with Miss Bewley. Do not come out until you hear the bell for supper. We will move Mary Ann to the infirmary."

Eliza grabbed Helen's hand. "Don't worry. Dr. Whitman will care for Mary Ann and we will pray."

9

Trouble Brewing

Mary Ann's fever abated somewhat but Eliza and Catherine still took turns sitting with her when she wasn't with Mrs. Whitman. Just as worry over Mary Ann eased, Helen Meek, little Salvijane Osborne, the three-year-old child of one of the emigrant families, and Louise Sager, the second to the youngest of the Whitman's foster children, fell ill. Soon many at the mission, including the entire Osborne family, were stricken.

"Mother, I should get up and help care for Helen and Louise, and the others." Mary Ann knew that once a person recovered, they wouldn't get measles a second time.

"No, I want you to be careful as you continue to get better," Mrs. Whitman told her, always mindful over her children. The infirmary continued to be full with very sick settlers.

• • •

Eliza woke early the morning of November 22 to find that her father had returned. He was talking with Dr. Whitman. She didn't want to interrupt, so she sat outside his infirmary door, patiently waiting.

When she realized she could hear them talking, she couldn't decide whether to stay or go. She'd have to walk through the infirmary were she to leave, disturbing the sick once again.

"It's beyond just dangerous, Marcus," she heard her father say to Dr. Whitman. What was beyond dangerous?

"I know. I just don't know what to do. We have seventy souls here more or less depending on us, and Narcissa and I can't possibly pick up and leave. Ten of the children are ours."

"The Cayuse are dying in staggering numbers. They are burying five or six people each day. They don't understand why the mission reports no deaths." Papa paused. "They somehow believe you are an evil medicine man—with powers such as they believe their healers have—and they blame you for the epidemic."

"I know. I know." Dr. Whitman sighed deeply. "They had the smallpox epidemic in the early years of our century, tuberculosis a decade or so later, and now this. What have we brought upon them?" He groaned. "They don't understand why our settlers get over this sickness and despite my ministrations their people continue to die. I've tried to explain that because they've never seen measles before, they had no defenses to fight it."

"But with Joc Lewis constantly stirring the pot, we can't possibly stem the tide of this growing hatred." Eliza's father paused. "I don't understand why they hate Narcissa so fiercely."

"After Narcissa lost Alice, she pulled into herself with grief. She no longer cared for the work here. Your mission at Lapwai brought pretty near an entire tribe to the Lord and here at *Wai-i-lat-pu*, we have one shaky convert. One." He shook his head. "When David, Helen, and Mary Ann came to our home, she found a reason to live again and she poured herself into them. And then the seven Sager children filled her nest to bursting. She loved being a mother again and seeing to the children's education and caring for the mission and the emigrants who pass through. She never had an admiration for the Cayuse, like you have for the Nez Perce. In caring for the house and children, she has lost her zeal, even her interest in working with the Cayuse. They sense it."

Eliza knew they were talking about Mrs. Whitman. When Dr. Whitman teased with her, he called her Mrs. Whitman or Mother, but when he worried, he called her Narcissa. Lately, he used her first name too often.

"I've heard mutterings. They say they have shared their land, their resources, and all they have with you, and yet you keep all your possessions strictly to yourselves." Papa carefully kept any criticism out of his voice.

"It's true. We believed it important to teach them to develop their own resources, to plant, harvest, and not be dependent on settlers. I see now that was wrong. I wish I had been a brother to them, not a stern authority."

Papa didn't respond.

"I've told the Cayuse leaders that if they want us to leave the territory, we will. We'd turn the mission over to Father Brouillet from up at the St. Anne mission to serve the Cayuse, since he's been the one they turn to for spiritual help. So far, I've had no answer."

"Marcus, I don't think the elders want you gone. It is a band of discontents, led not by a Cayuse but by Joe Lewis, who wants the mission grounds and possessions for himself."

"That's true. The men running the gristmill and butchery say that he skulks around, even during daylight. It used to only be at dusk and during the night. It's as if he is taking stock of everything we have." He stayed silent for a long while. "Henry, I don't know what to do to stave off trouble."

"Let's go and talk to the Cayuse elders and see if we can come to some understanding. I hate to take you away in the middle of an epidemic, but we must get to the bottom of all the rumors."

"Yes. Far better than to sit here with folded hands, doing nothing. I'll need to turn around quickly, however, and return to help Narcissa and to care for the sick. Perhaps you can stay longer and try to untangle this."

"Indeed. While we are gone, I want Eliza to mingle with the Cayuse who loiter nearby. They'll not pay attention to a small child, let alone a girl, and because she will be the only one on the mission property who can understand and speak Cayuse, she will be our eyes and ears."

Eliza couldn't help but be proud of the faith her father had in her. She heard the door open. Her father smiled when he found her sitting on the chair by the door. He swung her up to give her a proper hug.

"Sweet 'Liza, how good it is to see you looking well. I'm guessing you heard most of that conversation so there will be no need to repeat it."

She blushed and started to explain but her father stopped her. "I understand. You came to greet me and didn't want to interrupt. That's fine. Besides, it's far too late for secrets. Are you in agreement with working as our eyes and ears while we are away? You can then tell Dr. Whitman all you've heard on his return in a day or so."

"Yes, Papa. If Helen Meek is feeling well enough, perhaps she can join me and it will look as if we are playing. The Cayuse know Joseph Meek and respect him. They know Helen is his daughter. She will be safe."

Her father and Dr. Whitman rode off very early the next morning. Mrs. Whitman watched them until they were out of sight. The rye grass seemed to whisper farewells long after they were gone.

● ● ●

Eliza and Helen borrowed rag dolls from two of the Littles and borrowed needles and thread from Mrs. Whitman. They took out the scrap basket and picked out enough scraps of fabric to last them a good long time.

Mrs. Whitman gave them two large pairs of sewing scissors. "Tuck these in the sides of the baskets where you can reach them quickly in case of trouble." She looked worried as she squeezed Eliza's hand and kissed Helen on the forehead.

"We'll be fine, Mother," Helen said. "We're just going out to play dolls." She grinned at her mother but nothing seemed to wipe the fear off Mrs. Whitman's face.

"If you start to feel weak or sick again, Helen, come inside. One of the other girls can join Eliza."

The two settled themselves on the wooden bench near the door. It was fortunate the weather was unusually mild for November. A warm woolen shawl draped over their shoulders sufficed. Next to the bench stood an empty crate, and Eliza pulled it in front of them to serve as a worktable of sorts.

Just as they began to cut fabric for doll bonnets, a group of young Cayuse came from the gristmill carrying their bags of flour. They stopped by the front of the mission as usual to talk with each other before getting on their horses to go back to the village. Eliza saw from a quick glance that one man looked at them briefly, but dismissed them just as quickly.

"The elders won't listen to us," the shortest one said in Cayuse. "Each time we come to the mission it seems they charge us more for grinding our grain."

Helen glanced at Eliza to see if she understood. Eliza gave a barely perceptible nod. Helen couldn't understand a word of their language.

"Joe Lewis say the sickness caused by medicine doctor gives to our people." This man scuffed his moccasin-clad foot on the dirt and the dust he stirred up nearly made Helen cough. Because she didn't want to draw any attention she managed to swallow the cough into a tiny throat-clearing sound.

With the bonnets cut, the girls slid the scissors into the side of the basket closest to each of them and took up the needles and thread.

"Tomahas say his grandfather, who was sick unto death and had not long to live anyway, volunteered to test medicine, to seek truth." This man spoke with a clear voice that made the language easier for Eliza to hear. "Then they know for certain if it poison as Joe Lewis says." The man leaned in closer. "The grandfather drink vial of medicine in front of Tomahas. Two days later, he dead."

The men were silent. They shuffled around, clearly shaken by this news. Eliza longed to point out that if the grandfather was already near to death, couldn't the death have just been natural?

"That is why our people die and white people live. The white people get medicine. Our people get poison."

The short man had hardly finished saying that when the door to the mission opened and Mrs. Whitman came out holding the still body of little Salvijane Osborne who had died that morning of measles.

Eliza knew what she was trying to do. They'd heard the Cayuse grumblings about their people dying and the settlers recovering. She must have thought this would show them that the settlers experienced deaths as well. Tears ran down Mrs. Whitman's face. Mrs. Osborne stood behind her with her apron pulled over her face.

Eliza wished Mrs. Whitman had understood that these men were too worked up to care about a tiny girl, who to them was unimportant. One by one each man broke into a smile. A deep moan escaped Mrs. Whitman's throat and she backed into the mission house as Mrs. Osborne slammed the door. Tensions were high and this hadn't helped.

Eliza knew that if she had shown the body to the elders of the tribe, they would have mourned with her. These young men were not like the Nez Perce or even those Cayuse back in the village. These were the angry young men, whipped into discontent by Joe Lewis. These were like the men she had seen long ago, when she and Henry were gathering greens for Christmas, and like the one who stood over the women digging camas in Matilda's field. Angry, frightened men. Their world was changing.

She silently reached out and took Helen's hand, joining their prayers together.

10

No Time for Farewell

November 1847
Sexliwal—Season of Leaves

Eliza sat on a small stool in Dr. Whitman's office with the doctor, Mrs. Whitman, and two of the emigrant men. She had just finished telling them of all she'd overheard. Most of it was just more anger and discontent.

"We heard serious complaints from the elders as well. They did not say they wanted us to leave, but I think we must put the question to the mission board." Dr. Whitman sounded discouraged. "The death toll continues in the village. Measles have decimated the tribe. The mistrust of the settlers and the mission grows."

"Did the visit help at all?" Mrs. Whitman asked.

"If listening to their complaints helped, but nothing was resolved in the time I was there. Eliza's father stayed to see if they could find a solution; however, it is not with the elders and the families in the village that I am most concerned." He ran his hand shakily through his hair. "It's Joe Lewis and this group of young men who most concern me."

"Which young men?" asked Mr. Hall.

"As far as I know, Tomahas; the chief's two sons, Clark and Edward; Cupup-Cupup; Isiaasheluckas; Kiamasumkin; Tamsucky; Tolokite; and Wai-e-cat."

"Has it come far enough that we should arm ourselves?" Mrs. Whitman asked.

The doctor was silent for a long time. "No. We have never resorted to weapons in all the years we've been here. Besides, we have our hunting rifles." He sighed. "If we were to kill a Cayuse who'd never known the Lord . . ." He didn't finish his thought. "If we were to die it would be different. I recall the words of Paul, 'For to me to live is Christ, and to die is gain.'"

"I don't like to think of it, but I do look forward to seeing my Alice Clarissa again someday," Mrs. Whitman said wistfully.

"Enough of imagining the worst. Mr. Spalding may come up with a wonderful compromise." Dr. Whitman turned to Eliza. "Will you help us in this? I wish we had made a greater effort to learn the Cayuse language, but will you be our ears and keep me informed?"

Before she could answer, Mrs. Saunders stuck her head in the door and whispered, "The chief is here, Doctor, and insists on seeing you. He won't leave until he speaks with you."

"Please, show him in." Dr. Whitman sounded impatient.

It was Stickus, the Cayuse chief who lived on the Umatilla River. He spoke in English. "Stickus come to warn. Bad Indians kill doctor. Truth. Go." He shot his hand out toward the door. "Go. Go now." Without any more explanation, he left.

Mrs. Whitman began to cry.

"It is a warning indeed, Narcissa, but I don't believe it is imminent. Mr. Spalding is still with most of the Cayuse chiefs." His words were calm but he seemed agitated. "We must take time to prepare for a journey. It would be foolish to attempt now with winter coming on. We shall leave in the spring."

"Truly, Marcus?" Mrs. Whitman clung to his arm. "Back to Prattsburgh?"

"We'd have to report to the Mission Board, but yes, Prattsburgh."

• • •

The following Monday, November 29, dawned dark and gloomy, typical late autumn weather. The children who were well enough were back in the schoolroom. Eliza walked over to the gristmill to see if there were any Cayuse there with their late harvest. She carried a small bag of grain so that it would seem she had a purpose other than eavesdropping.

"I haven't seen a single Cayuse face today. Not one. Mighty strange, if you ask me," the miller said, pushing his hat up to scratch his forehead.

Strange indeed. She walked over to the butchery. Any day they were butchering, Cayuse men often came in. If they helped, they would get a cut of meat to take home. When she asked, the butcher shook his head. "Not nary a helper today. I'm trying to heft this beef all by myself. This is Monday, yes?"

She walked all around the mission and saw no one, so she went into the parlor where the doctor was reading. She reported that no one was on the mission property at all.

"Then why don't you go back to the schoolroom? Looks like you get a day off."

Eliza was slow to go back to the schoolroom. If she dawdled she'd miss arithmetic drills. Before she had time to circle the Indian Room, she heard glass break. She looked into the kitchen and saw Mrs. Whitman, who had been pouring milk for the sick children. Around her, acting menacingly by pushing and grabbing things, were eight or nine of the Cayuse that Stickus had called "bad Indians."

"Get out!" Mrs. Whitman shrieked. "Get out of here right now!"

"We need medicine. Get doctor. We go when we get medicine." It was Tomahas, the one whose grandfather died.

Dr. Whitman came in, bringing several vials and medicine and signaled Mrs. Whitman to back out. She, Eliza, and the girls who were sick could hear loud, angry voices and the soft voice of Dr. Whitman. It went on for a long time until they heard what sounded like a rifle explosion. They strained to see and they saw the doctor slump to the ground.

Eliza could feel her heart beating. She and Mary Ann helped the sickest children and pushed and prodded them back into the schoolroom. As she came back to get one of the babies, she saw Joe Lewis raise a gun and shoot Mrs. Whitman.

Her mouth was so dry she couldn't swallow. She grabbed the baby and went running back to the schoolroom. Mary Ann had told them what she'd seen. Two of the big boys took boards off the ceiling and hoisted the children up into an unfinished attic of sorts.

Eliza didn't know how long they were there but she would never forget the sounds of destruction, breaking glass, screams, yells, angry Cayuse threats. Doctor and Mrs. Whitman were gone. She didn't think their children were aware except Mary Ann. She didn't want to think of it, but as she prayed, she remembered them talking of holding their Alice Clarissa again. They didn't have to worry any longer. They were in the arms of Jesus.

Keeping the children quiet when they were so frightened took every bit of energy. The Uppers helped the children mouth the Bible verses they had memorized. Not a sound came out of their mouths, but the power of God's Word didn't need sound. It resonated in their hearts and helped calm them.

Some of the Littles and even Middles fell asleep. They were all hungry. It sounded like most of the intruders had gone outside. Mr. Saunders, John, and Francis opened the boards and slid down to have a look around. They didn't come back. Hours seemed to go by and the Littles were getting so hungry there were tears and they could no longer keep everyone quiet.

Eliza heard a shout from the schoolroom in Cayuse. "They know we are up here. They will be taking us down. Can I recite one verse before we go? 'But the God of all grace, who hath called us unto his eternal glory by Christ Jesus, after that ye have suffered a while, make you perfect, stablish, strengthen, settle you.'" Elizabeth and Helen hugged her as they heard the boards of the roof being taken down.

Eliza shouted down to them in Cayuse, "Are you going to kill us?"

They answered back in the same language. "We do not kill women and children. It is a dishonor."

"Mrs. Whitman was killed. She was shot."

"Not by Cayuse. She was killed by Joe Lewis. He dishonored himself and his people, both white and Delaware."

She turned back to the rest of those in the attic. "Be brave. It sounds like there is destruction below, broken glass, and possibly more. Do not look around, keep looking up to heaven. But they give their word they will not kill us. We will need to wait for rescue."

The children came down and two of the Cayuse men herded them out the schoolroom door to the emigrant house. One of the men told Eliza, "It is because we are going to burn the mission house."

Eliza didn't believe him. All the food, tools, and things they would need if the intruders planned to keep them here were in the mission house.

The big girls and some of the emigrant women were already

making a meal. No one talked. The shock of the day had been too much.

As Eliza lay on a blanket on the floor with Elizabeth and Helen, she couldn't help but worry about her family. Joe Lewis kept talking in Cayuse, saying this was only the beginning. They would clear all white settlers off Cayuse property. Later he said it was already taking place. As the evening wore on, he continued bragging and talking more and more. She could see the Cayuse looking at each other in uncertainty.

Papa was somewhere between the village and the mission. *Please, heavenly Father, keep him safe. If he knows what took place here today, keep him from taking dangerous risks to get here. Be with the Sager children, David, Helen, and Mary Ann, who lost both their parents today. And Lord, somehow let Your will be done.*

She wondered if God wept at such evil.

11

The Long Goodbye

December 1847
Haoq'oy— Season of Expectant Doe

Eliza often talked about making history, but she never thought this terrible loss would mark a turning point. It was several days until they learned the awful toll of that explosion of anger. Besides Dr. and Mrs. Whitman, eleven men were also killed. The intruders continued to hold all those in the emigrant house hostage.

Eliza often heard them talking among themselves. Now that their anger had played itself out, they didn't know how they could get out of this. It would be foolish to think that someone, soldiers maybe, would not be coming to seek retribution and to free the captives.

The next day Father Brouillet came riding up. He had gone to the Cayuse village and heard of what had happened. He didn't even get off his horse but called for two or three men from the village to come with him to the mission.

When they rode up to the emigrant house and dismounted, Father Brouillet could not speak, viewing the devastation. Eliza, too, froze upon seeing one of the Cayuse riding Tashe, Papa's horse. Did that mean that her father was also dead? Nobody seemed to have an answer, and the horseman just said he found Tashe wandering. That sounded unlikely.

No one had buried the dead. Father Brouillet gathered everyone around. He held a service for the dead and then had the men help him dig a grave for burial and wrap the bodies into winding sheets. Catherine, Eliza, and Elizabeth found the now-broken china doll that had been Alice Clarissa's and gently placed it in Mrs. Whitman's arms before they sewed the sheet closed.

Those were sad days. Without Dr. Whitman there to care for the ill, some of the sick children became worse. Hannah Sager died and it was soon apparent that Helen Meek was getting weaker and weaker. Elizabeth and Eliza took turns feeding and caring for her, but she slipped away one night.

A few days after, there was a knock at the door to the emigrant house. Strange. The Cayuse didn't knock. They just came in. The door opened and Eliza screamed. "*Piimx*!" Timothy stood at the door and folded her into his arms.

"Little One!" This usually stoic Nez Perce elder hugged her tightly to him. He spoke Nez Perce and told her that her mother had sent Eagle and him to find out what they could about her and her father.

"You still haven't seen my father?" Eliza couldn't help herself. Up to that minute she hadn't cried but it was as if it had all been saved up. Timothy awkwardly took the edge of her apron and wiped her eyes.

"Do not worry for your father. Much loved by Nez Perce and we pray for him just as we pray for you."

The whole time they spoke, the Cayuse watched him with suspicion. The two languages were close enough that they could make out the gist of the conversion.

"One of the men over there, helping with the burial, rode in on Tashe. That means if Papa is alive, he is on foot," she whispered to Timothy. "He says he found her wandering by the river."

"I talk to him and to Cayuse who hold you here. Tell them that I will take you home to your mother and to Nez Perce who love you."

Timothy talked to both men for a long time before he came back to her. She could see that he did not have good news. "They will not let you go. They fear punishment and believe they need all hostages to bargain, especially you." He continued in his language. "You are their only translator and their English not good enough to bargain or give orders to hostages. They say if I try escape with you, they hunt us down, no matter how far we get. I not have to finish the threat."

She sighed, but she was not sure she could leave anyway if Elizabeth and the others were still held hostage.

He moved her a little farther from any ears that might have been eavesdropping and lowered his voice to a whisper, so it sounded as if he were praying with her. "Word spread. Everyone knows what happened. News traveling. Hudson's Bay Company gathering goods and money for trade. Peter Ogden at Fort Vancouver planning to move all white settlers to fort, including your family. We all meet up at Fort Walla Walla for long trip along Columbia River to Fort Vancouver. Even now he finds boats and boatmen to accomplish this."

Eliza could feel the first little tingle of hope. If only Papa were safe.

"I can't stay with you, Little One. The Nez Perce moved your mother and family to safety in camp ten miles from Lapwai. We understand threat has grown. I need to go help her gather everything she need for journey to Vancouver. Matilda goes as well since there are two little ones who must be carried much of the way."

"I understand," she said. "I will pray that you find my father as you travel back to Lapwai. Godspeed, dear friend."

And with that, he was gone.

● ● ●

It was more than a month before the forty-seven survivors were rescued. During that time, Eliza was the interpreter. She had to translate every command. The constant worry for her family and sickness among the children, along with the loss of her friend Helen Meek, weakened her as well.

When Commander Peter Ogden finally arrived at the mission, he pulled Eliza aside. "Your family, including your father, are safe. He didn't dare come down to *Wai-i-lat-pu* because of angry Cayuse crisscrossing the whole area. The entire tribe are afraid of retribution from soldiers they heard were coming from Fort Vancouver, and were in an uncertain state." He shook his head. "Your father, not knowing what had happened to you, had to walk all the way, on foot and shoeless, from the Cayuse village to the Nez Perce encampment near Lapwai with no food and little water. It was a six-day journey, but happily he made it, and his Nez Perce friends treated his feet and fed him until he could meet up with the family."

Eliza found out they'd had to leave nearly everything behind and were on their way to Fort Walla Walla. It would be a hundred-mile trek during the worst of winter, but an entire party of Nez Perce were traveling with them for protection. Matilda carried two-year-old Martha, and Mama and Henry took turns carrying baby Amelia, both wrapped in buffalo robes for warmth. Timothy rode beside Papa. Another group of Nez Perce were staying at the Lapwai mission to protect it. Eliza knew that the mission, the printing press, and the gristmill would be in the good hands of the faithful Nez Perce congregation. The Lord's work would continue without the Spalding family.

It took Commander Ogden many hours to negotiate with the Cayuse. They had heard rumors that a company of soldiers was on its way. They wanted to hold the hostages to use them as shields between the soldiers and the Cayuse killers. Finally, the commander convinced them that it would be far better for them to take the goods in trade—a kind of ransom—blankets, ammunition, tools, and about four hundred dollars in exchange for the hostages, and separate and go into the wilderness to hide. He knew they were not likely to leave the rich holdings of the Whitman mission but the argument worked.

The hostages were loaded onto the wagons the commander had brought and made the slow thirty-mile journey to Fort Walla Walla.

As they pulled up to the gate at the fort, Eliza could see her mother and father, brother, and sisters along with Matilda and Timothy and many other Nez Perce faces she loved, including Noah, holding the reins of Eliza's beloved Ayi. Tired and weak, she managed to get off the wagon and run to her family. With tears and hugs and everyone talking at once, they moved to the barracks. After a warm meal, each one told their separate stories of what had happened when they were apart. Papa prayed with all the hostage families, and children who'd lost their parents were folded into other families.

As the fire died down, Eliza sat very close to Matilda. She took out her buffalo skin bag which, along with her journal, pen, and paints, was one of the few things left to bring. "*Kat'sa,* I have a gift for you." She took out her sampler and Matilda studied it.

"It is beautiful, *Miya.*" Her fingers touched the embroidered white man reaching out to the dark man and then traced the words: blessed are the peacemakers.

"You, Eliza. You are that peacemaker."

Eliza knew that life had changed forever, but she also knew that the Nez Perce treasured their Book of Heaven and had firmly embraced the faith that endures.

Afterword

After the Whitman Massacre, the mission board back in the States decided to close the work at Wai-i-lat-pu and Lapwai. The Spalding family stayed at Fort Vancouver for a short time but eventually traveled to the Willamette Valley to settle on a claim there. Eliza's father taught school. Eliza's mother, Eliza Hart Spalding—one of the first two white women to travel west of the Continental Divide—died there a little more than three years after leaving Lapwai of what may have been tuberculosis. Eliza was thirteen.

The work the Spaldings began in Lapwai continues. Visitors to the Nez Perce Museum and Visitors Center can walk along a path and see the Spalding Church—still in use today. Eliza would be pleased to know that 175 years later a flourishing community of believers still thrives among the Nez Perce.

In the story, the Nez Perce learn about the White Man's Book of Heaven from William Clark but that is only one theory. They may have first seen the Bible in the hands of a French trapper, a priest, or a Hudson's Bay trader. The fact that the four who traveled to St. Louis were in search of General Clark lends credence to the theory that it was during the Lewis and Clark expedition that they first learned about the Bible. Regardless of where they first saw it, that Bible roused a hunger in them for more of the Word of God.

In the nineteenth century and well into the twentieth century the word used to describe all the tribes of Native Americans was Indians. I've tried to avoid that wherever I could, using their own names for their people.

Almost all of those in the story were real people. Old Timothy and Matilda were very much real characters—beloved by the Spaldings—but Noah was a composite of many of the Nez Perce friends Eliza had. The Sager children and all those at the Whitman mission were taken right from history.

A few details were taken out of chronology—Eliza may have gone to the mission school for a short time in 1846, rather than for the first time in 1847. I have the school first open in September, to let us get to know some of Eliza's friends better. It actually opened in November of that year—hence Winter School. Too many children helped with harvest to start school any earlier.

President Polk decided that the men responsible for the massacre would be tried. It took two years to find them, and history is not clear whether those responsible were the ones who were put on trial. It is said that five "volunteers" from the tribe went on trial and were convicted. Joe Lewis was not one of those volunteers. One account states that he was killed in 1860 while robbing a stagecoach.

Eliza lived from 1837 until 1919. When she was a girl her mother would talk about life "back in the States." She never moved from the Oregon territory though she did live to see Oregon, Washington, and Idaho all achieve statehood. In her lifetime, she went from being a pioneer in an uncharted wilderness—the first non-native child to grow up in the Oregon territory— to seeing telephones, automobiles, traffic lights, and refrigerators.

Until the day she died, Eliza still loved her Nez Perce friends. In her seventies, she made a trip back to Lapwai. Here's what she said: "When we arrived at Lapwai there was such a feeling of sacredness. . . . There was a little cemetery and my father's grave, there was the spot where the house had stood. The bluffs, the river, the hills, where my brother and myself often played. It was no wonder that I would look and look. It seemed as if hardly a stone had been misplaced."*

---

* Eliza Spalding Warren, *Memoirs of the West: The Spaldings* (Portland, OR: Press of the Marsh Printing Company, 1916), 42.

Recipes

Old Scripture Cake with Syrup

(source unknown)

You'll find the translation at the end of the recipe. Enjoy!

Ingredients:

¾ cup Genesis 18:8

1½ cups Jeremiah 6:20

5 Isaiah 10:14 (separated)

3 cups sifted Leviticus 24:5

3 teaspoons 2 Kings 2:20

3 teaspoons Amos 4:5

1 teaspoon Exodus 30:23

¼ teaspoon each 2 Chronicles 9:9

½ cup Judges 4:19

¾ cup chopped Genesis 43:11

¾ cup finely cut Jeremiah 24:5
¾ cup 2 Samuel 16:1
Whole Genesis 43:11

Directions:

Cream Genesis 18 with Jeremiah 6.

Beat in yolks of Isaiah 10, one at a time. Sift together Leviticus 24; 2 Kings 2; Amos 4; Exodus 30; and 2 Chronicles 9.

Blend into creamed mixture alternately with Judges 4.

Beat whites of Isaiah 10 till stiff; fold in.

Fold in chopped Genesis 43; Jeremiah 24; and 2 Samuel 16.

Turn into 10-inch tube pan that has been greased and dusted with Leviticus 24.

Bake at 325 degrees F until it is golden brown or Gabriel blows his trumpet, whichever happens first. Bake for an hour and ten minutes. Remove from oven. After fifteen minutes, remove it from the pan. Cool completely. Drizzle some Burnt Jeremiah syrup over it.

Burnt Jeremiah Syrup

Ingredients:

1½ cups Jeremiah 6:20
½ cup Genesis 24:45
¼ cup Genesis 18:8

Directions:

Melt Jeremiah 6 in a heavy skillet over low heat. Keep cooking it till it is a deep gold, then add Genesis 24. Cook till smooth and remove from the heat. Add Genesis 18 and stir till it melts, then cool.

After drizzling this on the Scripture cake, you can decorate it with whole Genesis 43.

Translation

Genesis 18:8: "And he took **butter**, and milk, and the calf which he had dressed, and set it before them."

Jeremiah 6:20: "To what purpose cometh there to me incense from Sheba, and the **sweet cane** from a far country?" (Sugar)

Isaiah 10:14: "And my hand hath found as a nest the riches of the people: and as one gathereth **eggs** that are left, have I gathered all the earth."

Leviticus 24:5: "And thou shalt take **fine flour**, and bake twelve cakes thereof."

2 Kings 2:20: "And he said, Bring me a new cruse, and put **salt** therein."

Amos 4:5: "And offer a sacrifice of thanksgiving with **leaven**, and proclaim and publish the free offerings." (Baking powder)

Exodus 30:23: "Take thou also unto thee principal spices, of pure myrrh five hundred shekels, and of sweet **cinnamon** half so much."

2 Chronicles 9:9: "And she gave the king an hundred and twenty talents of gold, and of **spices** great abundance." (A dash of allspice and a dash of ginger)

Judges 4:19: "And he said unto her, Give me, I pray thee, a little water to drink; for I am thirsty. And she opened a bottle of **milk,** and gave him drink."

Genesis 43:11: "Carry down the man a present, a little balm, and a little honey, spices, and myrrh, nuts, and **almonds**."

Jeremiah 24:5: "Thou saith the LORD, the God of Israel; Like these good **figs**, so will I acknowledge them that are carried away captive of Judah, whom I have sent out of this place into the land of the Chaldeans for their good."

2 Samuel 16:1: "And when David was a little past the top of the hill, behold, Ziba the servant of Mephibosheth met him, with a couple of asses saddled, and upon them two hundred loaves of bread, and an hundred bunches of **raisins**."

Genesis 24:45: "And before I had done speaking in mine heart, behold, Rebekah came forth with her pitcher on her shoulder; and she went down unto the well, and drew **water**: and I said unto her, Let me drink, I pray thee."

KEY WORDS from the OLD SCRIPTURES: butter, sweet cane, eggs, fine flour, salt, leaven, sweet cinnamon, spices (allspice, ginger), milk, almonds, figs, raisins, water.

Pemmican Recipe
(courtesy of the USDA Forest Service)

You can make something very much like pemmican at home.
Try this recipe:

1 cup beef jerky, very finely shredded
½ cup dried cranberries or cherries, chopped
¼ cup unroasted sunflower seeds
2 tablespoons peanut butter, melted
1 tablespoon butter, melted

Mix everything together and form it into small balls or flattened cookie shapes. Chill in refrigerator overnight.

Glossary

Ayi—The Nez Perce word for little sister. It is also the name Eliza chose for her pony.

Camas—A plant from the asparagus family. The bulb was an important food source for both the Nez Perce and the Cayuse. It was somewhat like the sweet potato, only much sweeter.

Continental Divide—In North America, the Continental Divide separates the rivers that flow into the Pacific Ocean and those that flow into the Atlantic Ocean.

Curvet—A light leap by a horse, in which both hind legs leave the ground just before the forelegs are set down.

Digestive flux—We might now call this stomach flu or food poisoning. Its symptoms are upset digestive system, vomiting, and diarrhea.

Éehe—*Yes*, or *I agree* in Nez Perce.

Fortnight—An old term meaning two weeks. Literally means fourteen nights.

Frisket—The frisket is used in letterpress printing. It is a piece of parchment or oiled paper with a square cut out of the middle the exact size of the printing on the page. It keeps ink from getting on the borders of the printed page.

H'co-a-h'co-a-h'cotes (Black Eagle)—One of the three Nez Perce men who traveled to St. Louis to find out more about the White Man's Book of Heaven (the Bible). He fell ill and died in St. Louis.

http://www.museumsyndicate.com/item.php?item=45801

Hee-oh-'ks-te-kin (Rabbit-Skin Leggings)—One of the three Nez Perce men who traveled to St. Louis to find out more about the White Man's Book of Heaven (the Bible). On the way back to the Nez Perce nation he and No Horns on His Head were passengers on a steamboat with the famous painter George Catlin who painted portraits of both. Not too long after he arrived home he was attacked and killed by Blackfeet warriors.

Hinonoeino—The name by which the Arapaho tribe refers to itself meaning "our people."

Hin-mah-too-yah-lat-kekht—The boy called Joseph, son of Joseph the Elder, who in 1871 would become the now-famous Chief Joseph. 1840–1904.

Iceye'ye—*Coyote* in Nez Perce.

Ka-ou-pen (Man of the Morning)—A Flathead (Salish) who accompanied the three Nez Perce men to St. Louis. He fell ill and died in St. Louis.

http://photobucket.com/images/chief%20joseph/

Kat'sa—*Maternal grandmother* in Nez Perce.

Lenape—The name by which the Delaware referred to themselves, meaning "the people."

Lewis and Clark beads—The explorers knew it was important to bring gifts or trade goods for the native peoples. They brought beads, mostly from glassblowers in Europe. Many of the beads we find on native crafts come from those first beads. Here's what the explorers brought (*mace* is a phonetic spelling of *mease*, which is a measurement):

    5 pounds of white wampum (beads made from shells)
    5 pounds of glass beads, mostly small
    20 pounds of red glass beads, assorted
    5 pounds of yellow or orange beads, assorted
    2 cards of beads
    3 pounds of beads
    73 bunches of beads, assorted
    8½ pounds of red beads
    2 bead necklaces for young women

10 maces of white round beads for girls
2 maces of sky blue round beads for girls
3 maces of yellow round beads for girls
3 maces of red beads for girls
14 maces of yellow round seed beads for girls
5 maces of mock garnets*

Miya—*Child* in Nez Perce.

Nimiipuu—The name Nez Perce call themselves. It means "the people." (Nez Perce is the name trappers gave the tribe. It means "pierced nose" but it was given by mistake. Nez Perce never pierced their noses—that was a neighboring tribe, but the name stuck.)

Oregon territory—This area encompassed parts of present-day Idaho, Montana, Oregon, Washington, Wyoming, and British Columbia.

Oregon Trail—Covering over 2,000 miles, this trail started in Missouri and ended in Oregon City in Oregon territory, and from around 1843–1880 was the most popular way to travel to that area.

Pemmican—Much like our beef jerky of today.

Piimx—*Uncle* in Nez Perce.

Sampler—A needlework piece done most often by young girls in the eighteenth and nineteenth centuries. These are now considered historical treasures but their purpose was to teach embroidery skills. They often contain letters, numbers

---

* Elin Woodger and Brandon Toropov, "gifts," in *Encyclopedia of the Lewis and Clark Expedition* (New York: Facts On File, Inc., 2004), 158.

or numerals, the maker's name, age, and the date it was made, sometimes the school or academy and a favorite poem, saying, or Bible verse along with decorations.

Sandwich Islands—Now known as Hawaii, or the Hawaiian Islands, these islands were named by explorer James Cook in honor of the Earl of Sandwich. Captain Cook visited the islands in 1778.

Sarsaparilla—A soft drink similar to root beer.

Sham Battle—A pretend battle staged as part of a ceremony. Later performed in Wild West Shows by the Indians.

Used with permission.
http://digital.omahapubliclibrary.org/transmiss/congress/gallery/insh01.html

Service a la Russe—A new way of serving food, as opposed to French service (family style). Each dish is served one after another in its own separate course. Narcissa Whitman read as many family and housekeeping magazines of the day as she could find and kept trying to improve the gentility of her home.

Su-i-yap-po—Nez Perce name for *white men.*

Tats Meywi—*Good morning* in Nez Perce.

Photo above is public domain. Smithsonian.
http://commons.wikimedia.org/wiki/
File:No_Horn_on_His_Head.jpg

Tip-ya-lah-na-jah-nim (No Horns on His Head)—One of the three Nez Perce men who traveled to St. Louis to find out more about the White Man's Book of Heaven (the Bible). On the way back to the Nez Perce nation he and Rabbit-Skin Leggings were passengers on a steamboat with the famous painter George Catlin who painted portraits of both. On the way home he fell ill and died.

Travois—A sled-like device used by Native Americans to transport their teepees and household goods as they moved. It consisted of two poles lashed to either side of a horse. It had straps across so that the load could be lashed to it.

http://www.encyclopedia.com/topic/travois.aspx

Tule—Tall reeds that often grow in wetlands.

Tympan—In hand-operated letterpress, the tympan is the cloth or parchment stretched over the printing frame which is placed over the sheet to be printed.

Wai-i-lat-pu—The Whitman mission near Walla Walla, Washington. It literally means "the place of the people of the rye grass."

Yat'sa—*Older brother* in Nez Perce.

A classic work of literature, adapted for
children and beautifully illustrated.

John Bunyan's *The Pilgrim's Progress*, adapted for children and
beautifully illustrated. | *ISBN: 978-0-8024-2053-4*

Books for kids from   MOODY
                        Publishers®   *Books Kids Love and Parents Trust*

Adventures, friendships, and faith-testers . . . all
under the watchful eye of a great big God.

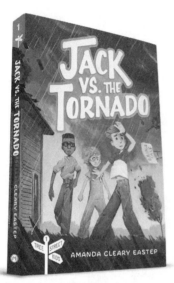

When Jack moves to the suburbs, can
he get back to his farm? Or is God up to
something else?

ISBN: 978-0-8024-2102-9

Can Jack and his friends protect his new puppy
from Fang, a creature of the deep woods?

ISBN: 978-0-8024-2103-6

Books for kids from   | *Books Kids Love and Parents Trust*

Daughters of the Faith Series

Ordinary Girls Who Lived Extraordinary Lives

Books for kids from  MOODY Publishers® | *Books Kids Love and Parents Trust*

Christian classics for kids from beloved author Patricia St. John

---

Rainbow Garden

A secluded garden in Wales becomes a surprise solace for Elaine, a little girl traveling far from her London home. | ISBN: 978-0-8024-6578-8

The Secret at Pheasant Cottage

Lucy has only known life with her grandparents at Pheasant Cottage. So what are her dim memories of something—*and someone*—else? | ISBN: 978-0-8024-6579-5

Star of Light

Hamid and his little blind sister attempt to escape their mountain village and the threat of losing each other in search of a new home. | ISBN: 978-0-8024-6577-1

The Tanglewoods' Secret

Ruth and her brother, Philip, find solace and adventure in the natural beauty and mystery of Tanglewoods. | ISBN: 978-0-8024-6576-4

Three Go Searching

When Waffi and David, a missionary doctor's son, find a sick servant girl and a mysterious boat, an exciting adventure begins. | ISBN: 978-0-8024-2505-8

Treasures of the Snow

After Annette gets Lucien into trouble at school, he decides to get back at her by threatening the most precious thing in the world to her: her little brother, Dani. But tragedy strikes first. | ISBN: 978-0-8024-6575-7

Where the River Begins

Ten-year-old Francis is taken in by a new family while his mother is terribly sick. There he discovers the source of both the nearby river and the Christian life. | ISBN: 978-0-8024-8124-5

Books for kids from  MOODY Publishers® | *Books Kids Love and Parents Trust*

Heroines Behind the Lines Series

ISBN: 978-0-8024-0576-0

ISBN: 978-0-8024-0577-7

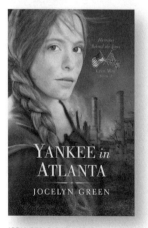

ISBN: 978-0-8024-0578-4

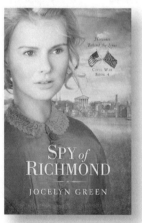

ISBN: 978-0-8024-0579-1

MOODY
Publishers®

From the Word to Life®